# The
# Least
# You
# Need
# to
# Know

SARABANDE BOOKS

# The
# Least
# You
# Need
# to
# Know

STORIES BY

# Lee
# Martin

1-3545

Copyright © 1996 by Lee Martin
First Edition
All Rights Reserved

No part of this book may be reproduced without written permission
of the publisher. Please direct inquiries to:

Managing Editor
Sarabande Books, Inc.
2234 Dundee Road, Suite 200
Louisville, KY 40205

Library of Congress Cataloging-in-Publication Data
Martin, Lee, 1955–
    The least you need to know : stories / by Lee Martin.
        p.        cm.
    Contents: The least you need to know — Light opera — The welcome
    table — Small facts — The end of sorry — Secrets — The price is the price.
    ISBN 0-9641151-2-3 (cloth). — ISBN 0-9641151-3-1 (pbk.)
    I. Title.
PS3563.A724927L43    1996
813 .54 — dc20        95-35647

Cover Painting: *Shadowed Door* by Marvin Cone
Reproduced by kind permission from:

Sheldon Memorial Art Gallery
University of Nebraska-Lincoln
Nebraska Art Association Collection
Nelle Cochrane Woods Memorial
1972.N-287

Cover and Interior Design by Tree Swenson

Manufactured in the United States of America
This book is printed on acid-free paper.

Sarabande Books is a non-profit literary organization.

ACKNOWLEDGMENTS

I am grateful to the following publications in which some of the stories in this collection first appeared: *New England Review,* "The Least You Need to Know"; *The Georgia Review,* "Light Opera"; *DoubleTake,* "The Welcome Table"; *Yankee,* "Small Facts"; *Glimmer Train Stories,* "Secrets"; *Prairie Schooner,* "The End of Sorry."

My thanks to the Bread Loaf Writers' Conference, the Nebraska Arts Council, the Ohio Arts Council, and the Tennessee Arts Commission for their support during the writing of these stories. Many thanks to Amy Bloom, Sarah Gorham, Joy Johannessen, Susan Ketchin, and Phyllis Wender. And to Hilda, Marly, Judy, Gerry, Ellen, Paul, and Sherry: my limitless gratitude for your encouragement, good friendship, and wisdom.

FOR DEB

# CONTENTS

# FOREWORD

I DON'T KNOW how one judges seven hundred collections
of short fiction. Astute readers helped screen out the illegible,
the incomprehensible, the ones who mistook this for a nonfiction
prize, or even for some other prize-winning event altogether, like
recipes. A hundred collections were pretty good. Ten were outstanding. Lee Martin's stuck out like evening's first star. I stopped
reading to search and began reading for pleasure, from my first
encounter with one of Martin's several, fiercely loving, utterly self-
absorbed and self-deceiving fathers to the wonderful, shameful
doings and brotherly love in Salktown, in "The Price Is the Price."

Although Lee Martin gracefully acknowledges the influences
(by which he means writers "who gave me permission to write
about the people I know best") of Bobbie Ann Mason, Richard
Ford, Tobias Wolff, and Bernard Malamud, his own distinctive
voice has the qualities of his favorite setting: the commonplace and
middle-class turned over with a searchlight of want and need to
know. Morticians and insurance men, salesmen and farmers;
women hoping to make life more beautiful and less pressing with

delicate, bewildering hobbies and necessary flirtations; boys who veer from shame to pride, from decency to irredeemable wrongs, in an afternoon; people who do not quite recover, during the time of our acquaintance, but do not give up gracefully.

Lee Martin's world is one of love gone true and astray, of power felt and misused and foolishly courted, and of forgiveness and the exhausting efforts towards happiness we cannot help making. Like rural Illinois and small-town Indiana, the land he comes from and writes about, his work has sudden beauty and a flat ugliness that's close to death, with very little that is merely pretty or trivial between those points.

Martin's work resists the pull of shiny look-at-me prose and *nostalgie pour la boue,* one the inevitable result of too many competent people being encouraged to show off their tricks and erudition as competitive sport, the other a dead-end mix of too much technique and too little heart. Martin wants to tell the story. He wants us to know everyone and give them a chance, to understand what is happening, even as we are shaking our heads at how appalling, how lame, how stupid, how vulnerable we all are.

I hear that Lee Martin's aunt let him know that she wasn't real happy with what he's done with some of the family stories, and I know, being the kind of man he is, that pains him as much as a good story pleases him. But having come to know Leon Silver and his smooth, hopeful ways and the art of egg blowing and painting, the complex, emotional language of cars and trucks, the irresistible distortions of family myths, I am more than happy. I am glad and grateful that he has so much to shape, and move and tell us.

AMY BLOOM
*July 1995*

The
Least
You
Need
to
Know

# THE LEAST YOU NEED TO KNOW

•　　•　　•　　•　　•　　•　　•　　•

**W**HEN I WAS a boy, my father cleaned up crime scenes. Murders, suicides: after the police had sorted everything out, he was the one the insurance companies called. "It's a hell of a thing," he told me once. "To see what I see. Believe me, Telly. You wouldn't want to know."

I was fifteen then, in 1961, and from time to time one of the hoodlums at my school would press me for details, and I would oblige, inventing *Police Gazette* stories of pulp and gore. My talent for spinning these lies disgusted me, but in those days, I was strictly Varsity Club — I ran track, practiced debate, sat on the student senate — and I used my father's job to win a hold with a crowd unlike my own. These were the boys who had never abandoned their ducktails and pompadours for the short bristles of crew cuts and flat tops. They were juvenile delinquents, my father said. Their lives, he assured me, would amount to squat.

But that didn't stop me from envying their sneers and

slouches, their motorcycle jackets, the very smell of them — Lucky Strikes and Vitalis. It was the scent of back seats and billiard parlors, of dark worlds I dreamed about, but never dared enter. There were limits, I suspected, to how far someone could travel into danger and come back healthy and whole.

The truth is I knew little about the work my father did or what it cost him. I only knew he waded into places and saw things most men wouldn't dare imagine, and because he did, he came to believe he had uncommon rights.

"Chum," he would say to some Joe at the hardware store. "Are you sure you want that linoleum? Wouldn't ceramic tile give you more pleasure? Of course, if it's shoddy you want . . ."

He would knock on strangers' doors: "Bub, why do you want to let your house go to pot? What would it cost you? A coat of paint? A little sweat? Think about it, friend. Is this the way you want to live?"

He had a theory that sloppy living led to cruel living. The way he saw it, if people would only keep their homes neat and orderly, they'd be less likely to subject them to mayhem. "A man who lies down in mud gets muddy," he said to me once. "Your grandfather taught me that. I've always remembered it, Telly. You should, too."

One night, in Joliet, we broke into a house. My father sprung the lock with a charge card, and, presto, we were inside. "No one home," he said. "We'll take a look, just a peek, see what's what."

In the kitchen, there was a sink full of dirty dishes. We washed them. We dried them and stacked them in the cupboards. We rinsed the sink and polished the faucets. We wiped the counter tops.

My father laid his arm across my shoulders. "There's no telling what we've kept from happening here," he said, impressing on me the nobility of our chore — how we had possibly prevented some act of violence. He put a finger to his lips. "Don't say a word. Keep it mum. No one has to know."

It would be a while before I would realize that something was snapping inside him, whatever it is that keeps us anchored to the true, sane parts of ourselves. Now it makes me shake my head to imagine how close we were to danger, but that night in a strange house, I was too full of our daring to mind the risk.

I kept wondering how this could be the same man who every night settled into his Barcalounger to listen to his record collection: Johnny Mathis, Nat King Cole, The Mills Brothers. "Isn't this fine, Telly?" He would close his eyes and hum along with "Glow Little Glow Worm." "Doesn't it make you glad you're alive to hear it?" How could this be the same man who only hours before had arranged his favorite Christmas ornament — four plastic blocks that spelled out N-O-E-L in green and red letters — with fussy precision on top of our television set. "Here we are," he had said. "Blessed indeed. We've got the joyous Christmas season, we've got stain-resistant carpet, we've got Perry-By-God-Como on the hi-fi."

The worst part about his job, he had told me, was the moment right before he walked into a house where some sort of brutality had taken place. "Picture this, Telly. I'm all alone. I have my hand on the doorknob, and I'm scared because I don't know what I'll find. It makes me think of the moment when what's going to happen hasn't yet, that moment just before someone takes a step and changes everything forever."

That night, as he pulled the panel truck into our drive, I saw my mother's shadow move across our living room drapes. I imagined the rightful owners returning to their home in Joliet. They would stand in their kitchen, in the overwhelming glare of light; they would gaze upon the miracle — clean dishes — and puzzle over how and when it had come.

THE NEXT day, I came home from school and found my mother sitting on the sofa with a man I didn't know. He was a handsome man with a wild shock of red hair. He had folded his duffle coat over the back of the sofa and had tossed his hat, a brown fedora, onto the coffee table. He was smoking, and every time he laughed, he bent at the waist and let his cigarette, its ash growing longer, dangle between his knees.

My mother had lit the Christmas candles on our fireplace mantle, and our living room smelled of tobacco smoke and bayberry. Outside it was cold and gray, and a fine sleet was peppering our windows. The air had left a taste of steel in my mouth and a burning ache in my throat and lungs. Nat King Cole's Christmas album was playing on my father's hi-fi, and when this stranger laughed, I could tell he was thankful for the warmth and shelter of our home.

"Oh, Telly," my mother said, reaching out her arms to me. Her fingers, long and elegant, curved up to her filed and polished nails. "Come say hello to Mr. Silver. He's been kind enough to drop by with some information about Costa Rica."

This was the year she wrote travel guides to countries she had never seen. Survival guides to distant lands, she called them — the least you need to know. They were thin paperbacks. No photos. Just a few brief paragraphs sketching out history, climate, lodging, points of interest — scant information garnered from encyclopedias, almanacs, hotel directories.

"Isn't this dishonest?" I asked her once.

She shrugged. "I borrow a bit here, a bit there. Nothing verbatim. God knows I would never do verbatim. I couldn't live with that."

That winter, she was working her way through Latin America.

"Where are we off to this time?" I had asked her that morning.

"Costa Rica."

"Via?"

"*Compton's World Book* and *National Geographic.*"

She spent her days in the reference room of the public library. She came home toward evening, when the light had started to fade, and sometimes, she sat on the window seat with her legs tucked beneath her, and when it was finally dark, and I had switched on a lamp, she would put her hand to her throat, and she would say, "Oh, Telly, it's you."

Mr. Silver stood and offered me his hand. "Leon Silver," he said. His skin was dry, and he smelled of old books, a musty smell of cloth bindings. The elbows of his corduroy jacket were shiny with wear, and one of his shirt cuffs was fastened with a safety pin. "As in Bells," he said, with a wink. "You know, 'Silver Bells.' "

"I know," I said. "My father plays it on his accordion."

"Mr. Clean plays the accordion?" He laughed, a deliberate

laugh — "Ha, Ha, Ha" — and I knew that he and my mother, at some time, had spoken about my father in a secretive, less than flattering way.

I wasn't sure how I felt about that. My father was, after all, my father, and despite his sometimes maddening obsession with order, he was, at heart, a sweet man, who wanted a pleasant life. Still, it wasn't easy being his son — "Mister, this is a sorry excuse for a room. Clean it up pronto. Savvy, Kemo Sabe?" — and without a certain tolerance on my part, I might have despised him.

He wasn't the sort of man people warmed to. At parties, he was either too forward — "this floor could use a coat of wax, chum" — or else he was off by himself, face to the wall, pretending to be studying the artwork. The only time he was really comfortable was when he was in the tidy perimeters of his own home. "Let's put on the glad rags," my mother would say to him from time to time. "Let's paint the town." After spending her days, reserved and bookish in the library, she was ready to cut loose. He was generally content in his Barcalounger, feet up, listening to his hi-fi.

"The accordion is a wind instrument." Leon Silver let his cigarette ash tumble to the carpet. "I bet you didn't know that. Most people think it's a string instrument like the piano, but it's not. It's a wind."

A few days before, at breakfast, my mother had said to me, "I've been having the strangest dream. Night after night. I dream that I'm in one of my countries, only it isn't me — you know how dreams are — it's someone who's supposed to be me, but much better looking, and this someone is lost, off the track somehow, but not to worry, she has one of my survival guides. The problem is, nothing is where the guide says it should be. She can't find her hotel. She can't catch a bus. And then your father shows up, only he's not your father. He's Groucho Marx, and when she asks him for directions, he says, 'Say the secret word' — you know, like Groucho does on his television program — but all she can say is 'Who's to blame here? Who's to blame?' And then this woman who is not your mother and this man who is not your father stand there in a foreign land and say nothing."

She was a cordial woman, slender, with beautiful hands. She had grown up on a farm downstate and had come north during the war to work in a munitions plant in Hammond. All day, she painted artillery shells, sometimes leaving her name and an outline of kissing lips in tiny script on the underside. Later, in her rooming house, she imagined how some soldier would see her name — *Dottie* — and would wonder who she was and what she looked like, and perhaps even conjure up a face, and a scent of gardenias, and carry it with him through the most horrid parts of the war.

On Saturday nights, she and the other girls in her rooming house went to the Royal-Joyo Dance Hall, and there she fell in love with my father, an accordion player in a polka band, a young man with black hair and a spangled vest. When she watched him play, she told me years later — when she watched him squeeze his accordion, run his fingers over its keys and buttons — she felt a series of small and delightful explosions fire along her spine. "A musician," she told me. "Can you imagine? I was gone on him.

Let me tell you, I was crazy in love with your father. A polka, Telly? You can't help but be happy."

I stared at Leon Silver's cigarette ash, its gray smudge on our carpet. My mother stared at it, too. Her eyes were wide open, and there was a tremor of a smile around her lips, as if she had caught sight of something she had never imagined she would see. Each Saturday, for years, she had vacuumed that carpet, retracing the same diagonal lines my father insisted gave the room symmetry and proportion. "Oh, you," she said to Leon Silver. She tapped a finger on the back of his hand. "You Mr. Smarty-Pants." She pulled me down on the sofa between them. "Mr. Silver is a reference librarian. If you ever want to know anything — I mean, anything, Telly — ask Leon."

Just then, we heard my father's panel truck rumble into the garage. For a long moment, the engine raced, a roar caged and amplified by the cement walls. When it stopped, a swift and vicious silence settled around us. My mother glanced at her watch. "Vic's home," she said. "What a surprise."

The moment he came into the living room, I knew something was wrong. He was still wearing the red coveralls he usually slipped out of in the garage, and there was a look on his face, puzzled, as if he had stumbled into the wrong house.

My mother smoothed her skirt over her lap. "Vic," she said. "Vic, sweetie, we have a guest."

Leon Silver reached across the coffee table. He snubbed out his cigarette in a saucer my mother must have brought him to use as an ashtray. He ran his hands through his red hair.

My father didn't acknowledge him. He stormed past him to

the hi-fi. I felt the floor shake beneath my feet. "Some people." He yanked the tone arm off the record, scratching the needle across the grooves. "Jesus, it makes me wonder."

"God, Vic, what is it?" my mother said.

He wouldn't turn and look at us. He was gripping the hi-fi cabinet with both hands, his shoulders lifted, his head hanging down. "No one's supposed to be there," he said, and his voice was soft and mellow the way, moments before, Nat King Cole's had been. "I mean, you expect a certain amount of unpleasantness in this line of work, but the one thing you never plan on is having someone there."

"Vic?" my mother said again.

He kept talking as if he were alone. He kept his head bowed, and his voice never varied, low and steady, somewhere between a chant and a prayer: "I'm doing this job on Laramie Drive, just a few blocks from here — a suicide, a young girl, shotgun blast to the head." The glow from the Christmas candles fell across his neck. "It's a mess: blood-soaked carpet, pieces of skin stuck to the ceiling and the walls. You've got to scrape that off. You've got to make it come clean. Any way you look at it, it's a chore."

Leon Silver leaned forward. "Say, that's not something you should talk about," he said. "That's not decent. Not in front of your wife and son."

My father turned and looked at him for the first time. He looked at him the way I imagined he must have regarded any stain, as if it were something he would have to remove. "Who is this?" he said to my mother. "For God's sake, Dottie, does he have to be here?"

"This is a friend of mine, Vic." Though I was next to her on the sofa, her voice sounded far away. "Leon Silver."

"Let me tell you, Mr. Silver. It's not easy what I do." My father reached into his coveralls and pulled out a piece of white enamel the length and shape of one of my mother's nail files. "Do you know what this is?" Leon Silver shook his head. "We call it a bone in the business. It's what I use to scrape up blood stains. I wet the stain with spotter and then I get down on my knees and start scraping. The blood foams up, and let me tell you, you don't forget the smell of blood — rotten — it stays with you." He tossed the bone toward the coffee table, and it landed on the crown of Leon Silver's fedora. "That's what I was doing when this girl's mother sat down on the floor beside me to watch." I felt Leon Silver press his shoulders into the back of the sofa. "Why would she want to do that, Mr. Silver? Can you answer me that?"

"No," said Leon Silver. "I don't know anything about that."

"That's right," said my father. "You don't know. But me, I'm there trying to do my job. It's a job someone has to do, right? And this woman is sitting there watching me scrape up her daughter's blood. Well, let me tell you, it gives me the willies, and after a while, I say to her — you know just to make conversation, just to try to make this bearable — I say to her, 'You might want to consider a different carpet for this room. Shag is all the rage right now, but, when you get down to it, a nice indoor-outdoor might be a better investment.' And she says to me, 'You cruel bastard. How can you be so insensitive? How can you do this job? You must be a sick man. You must be some sort of creep.' That's what she said. She didn't even know me, but she had made up her mind about me."

I listened to the sleet and imagined the cold outside. "I just want the best for people," my father said, and there was a catch in his voice. "Really, I do."

Leon Silver stood up. "You went ahead with the job? I can't believe you did that. You should have walked out. That would have been the decent thing."

My father took a step toward him. "Dottie, this isn't a good time for company." He started walking toward his Barcalounger on the other side of the room.

"No," she said, "I suppose not."

"What's this?" he said, stopping by the television set. "What in the hell kind of stunt is this?"

The N-O-E-L blocks had been rearranged to spell out L-E-O-N.

"That's just a joke, Vic," my mother said. "That's all."

"You're a funny guy," my father said. "Where do you live?"

"On Cicero," said Leon Silver.

"In one of those rooming houses?"

"That's right."

"Take your meals out or in your room?"

"In my room generally."

"Hot plate?"

"Yes."

Leon Silver's voice shrank as he answered my father, and I could tell he was ashamed of the life he had.

"Ever visit with the other tenants?" my father asked.

"Not often."

"No, I imagine not," my father said. "I imagine you're the kind most people avoid. I don't know how my wife hooked up with you."

He had never been a violent man, but I could see he wanted to harm Leon Silver.

"Vic," my mother said, her voice low with warning.

I don't know what he was thinking then, but I imagine he must have sensed that something was stretching thin, that if he went any further, it would snap, and then everything would come apart, fly into a mess he would never be able to put straight.

"You should know something," Leon Silver said.

My father raised his hand; he pressed his palm into the air before him. My mother was looking all about her, trying to get her bearings, as if she had found herself in a place she had never thought she would be. It was nearly dark outside, and the four of us were shadows in the candlelight. I sensed, even then, that a decision was about to be made, but that no one had the courage to make it. It would be years before I would understand that it had something to do with the violence we can do to love, and the will it takes to mend it. Then, I only wanted the lights to come on, to hear Nat King Cole crooning, to see my father, relaxed in his Barcalounger, letting the liquid tones wash him clean.

I went to Leon Silver and touched him on the arm. "You should go," I said, as kindly as I could. I felt the muscles in his arm tense and quiver, and then go slack, as if he were thankful someone had stepped forward to tell him what to do. Then, without a word, he gathered up his coat and hat, and disappeared from our home.

BUT THAT'S not the story I need to tell — at least, not all of it.

The girl on Laramie Drive was a girl named Ellen Hemp. She sat behind me in World History, and one day she laid a note on my desk. She was one of the spooks — that's what we called them — the unpopular kids we never saw. They eased themselves along the corridors, books hugged to their chests, their shoulders rounded in, trying to make themselves small. I felt the note at my elbow, and without turning around, I knew Ellen Hemp was waiting there behind me, chewing on her hair, her glasses slipped down on her nose.

Now I can imagine what it must have taken for her to have written that note, and how simple it would have been for me to have accepted it. But I was fifteen then, and when you are fifteen, you have no idea who you are; I couldn't bear to risk even the smallest part of myself. So I used my elbow to shove the note off my desk.

A few days later, Ellen Hemp was dead, and then, I saw her everywhere. Like the scratch my father left in the Nat King Cole album, her face would appear in my mind with regularity. And when it did, I would feel a skip, a catch, as if something were flipping over inside me, and then I would have to remember.

Years after my father had died, I would ask my mother if she had loved Leon Silver. "He made me feel freer," is all she would say.

That night, after he had gone, she brushed his cigarette ash from the carpet. She put the N-O-E-L letters back into their proper order.

My father dropped into his Barcalounger. "I wish I was somewhere else," he said. "Mexico or somewhere. Honest to God, Dottie. Anywhere a long way from here."

By New Year's, he would be in the psychiatric ward at the VA Hospital. There he would confess that the story of Ellen Hemp's mother had been a lie, that he had only imagined her presence beside him.

"Getting a few things sorted out," he would say whenever I would visit. "Putting a shine on, hey, Telly? The old spic-and-span."

At home one night I put a Perry Como record on the hi-fi, and my mother came in from the kitchen, and stood there, listening to the music. "For a minute, I thought Vic was here." She laid her hand on my head. "Don't be afraid of your life, Telly. You'll disappoint yourself with the things you'll do, but be patient. After a while, you'll swear it was someone else who did those things. Not you."

I let the record play to its end. Then I went to bed, and I lay awake a long time, trying to imagine the day my father would come home and life would start for us again.

The best part of his job, he always said, was leaving a house after everything was clean: "What keeps me going is thinking about years later, when it no longer matters who we were or what we did while we were alive. Someone else will live in that house, and if they're lucky, they'll never hear about the horrible thing that happened there."

That was the blessing he left them, he said, the one they would never know.

# LIGHT OPERA

• • • • • • • •

IN 1952, the year my mother feared she might lose me, she became the time and temperature voice on the telephone. The phone company selected her, after a nationwide search, because she had a bright voice with no discernable accent, and that meant her recorded messages could be distributed throughout the country. For a while, this gave her a certain status in our town; then, the novelty wore off, and she was again Lois Sievers, the undertaker's wife, who gave piano lessons to any pupils whose parents didn't mind marching them up the funeral chapel's steps.

She used her pretty voice to put her students at ease. "This is middle C," she told them at their first lessons. "We always begin with middle C."

When she spoke to my father, which she did less frequently in those days, she used a more severe tone — muted — as if over their years together, he had dulled her, as if he were a student who had sounded more flat notes than she could ever forgive.

On occasion, I dialed the time and temperature number just to hear her, and when I did, I thought she sounded like a woman I would one day enjoy meeting. What I'm saying is, you could do worse than to have that voice waiting for you at the other end of a call.

On Saturday afternoons, she listened to the Metropolitan Opera broadcasts with her friends, Mr. and Mrs. Pettyjohn, who preferred light opera to *opera seria*. The former, they said, offered them beauty and passion without any of the bother of life's gruesome tragedies.

Mr. Pettyjohn was a retired Army officer who served our town as night watchman; Mrs. Pettyjohn taught Latin at the high school. Once when I complained in her class about learning verb conjugations — bones of a dead language, I called them — she said to me, "Nothing of beauty ever dies. Once you know it, you know it. You carry it here inside you. *Aere perennius*. Translation, Mr. Sievers?"

I tried to stammer a reply, but she stopped me with a hand slapped down on her desk. "More lasting than bronze."

"Nothing lasts forever," I said. "People die."

"As long as one person knows *amo* . . . Mr. Sievers?"

"I love."

"*Amas?*"

"You love."

"*Amāmus?*"

"We love."

"Exactly, Mr. Sievers. Correct."

On those Saturday afternoons, in our living room above the

chapel, my mother made tea and served it in the china cups her grandmother had brought with her from Russia.

"Perry, you should read Turgenev," Mrs. Pettyjohn said to me once.

"Chekhov," said Mr. Pettyjohn.

They sat together on my mother's love seat, Mr. Pettyjohn with his teacup and saucer balanced on his knee, Mrs. Pettyjohn holding hers at her chin. Dostoevsky was too dreary, they both agreed.

"Don't waste your time on a gloomy Gus like him," said Mrs. Pettyjohn.

Said Mr. Pettyjohn, "As for Tolstoy, remember this, Perry. Never trust a man who doesn't worship his wife."

My mother, despite my father's objections, insisted on my presence those Saturdays. I sat across from the Pettyjohns on a ladder-back chair, ready to fiddle with the tuning knob on the Philco console whenever the broadcast began to fade. Over the airwaves, I listened to that afternoon's opera-goers taking their seats, to their murmured conversations punctuated by the sounds of the orchestra members tuning their instruments. When the master of ceremonies, Milton Cross, began to announce the prologue — "When the gold curtain rises, we'll see the wood nymphs frolicking in the forest" — Mr. and Mrs. Pettyjohn would set their tea aside and clasp hands.

"You can learn something from them," my mother had told me. "All these years and they still adore each other. A man shouldn't be afraid to wear his heart on his sleeve."

Sometimes during the opera, Mr. Pettyjohn would weep. He

would lay back his head, and his face would be shiny with tears.

"Good gravy," my father said when I divulged this bit of information. "A constable of this city. A municipal official. A man responsible for our well-being."

On occasion, Mr. Pettyjohn would be so taken with the music that his angina would seize him, and he would have to slip a nitroglycerin pill beneath his tongue.

Opera, my father said, was all wailing and caterwauling and far-flung drama. "A display," he said. "A spectacle. And on top of that, it's in some pig-Latin gibberish no one can understand."

"The language of love," my mother said. "The words don't matter, only what you feel when you hear them."

ONE SATURDAY, at the end of *Die Fledermaus*, Mrs. Pettyjohn said, "We should call your husband now."

"Roy?" my mother said.

"Yes. We need to call Roy."

One glance at Mr. Pettyjohn, and I recognized the dry, fixed stare of the dead. He seemed to be looking straight at me as if any minute he would tell me to switch off the Philco, but already I could see the muscles had stiffened in his jaws and a blue tinge had spread through his lips.

I stood up, fastening the button of my sports coat. "Don't worry, Mrs. Pettyjohn," I said, in the comforting voice I had learned from my father. "We'll take care of you."

THAT WINTER, my father had offered to make me his helper — to teach me what his father had taught him.

"There are things boys shouldn't be a part of," my mother had said. "Delicate boys."

I was sixteen then, and the last thing I wanted to be known as was a "delicate boy." So when my father started assigning me duties — doorman, parking attendant, floral arranger, pallbearer — I looked upon them as responsibilities that would distinguish me. He bought me a navy blue suit, black wingtips with rubber soles, a charcoal gray topcoat, and black gloves with a fedora to match.

"Listen to me, Perry," my mother said the first time she saw me in my new suit. "You should be careful. Believe me. I know. I want you to have friends. I want you to have a normal, happy life."

I learned my father's tools: scalpel, auger, trocar. Though he never allowed me in the embalming room, at times he would pass along some bit of information: how to fill the sunken areas on the backs of hands with injections of massage cream; how to shut a mouth by running a needle from the inside of the lower lip, in through a nostril, and back; how to lay cotton pledgets on the eyeballs before closing the lids.

My one distinction as a young man was the fact that my father was a mortician, and though I am ashamed to admit it now, I often betrayed his confidence and used those details to impress the boys I hoped would become my friends. For a time, I answered our phone with what I thought were jazzy greetings: "Sievers Funeral Home. You stab 'em, we'll slab 'em; you plug 'em, we'll plant 'em; you bag 'em, we'll tag 'em."

Then my father found out and demanded I stop: "Someday, when you take my place, everyone will know you. Rich and poor, handsome and plain. They'll come to you with their trouble and ask you to respect it. You'll have to make room in yourself for all the sorrow they'll bring you. You'll have to be an upright man, Perry. You'll have to be the kind of man people can trust."

The Saturday Mr. Pettyjohn died, I was trying to be that sort of man, noble and kind, so when my father asked me to fetch Sammy the Egg, I slipped on my overcoat and galoshes and went out into the cold night.

Sammy was the baldheaded barber who came, whenever my father called, to cut the corpse's hair. It was nearly eleven o'clock when we left his shop and made our way down Main Street to the funeral home, and Sammy kept singing "The Tennessee Waltz," a tune my mother played from time to time on the piano. He had a rich baritone voice, and despite the lateness of the hour, he allowed himself full throat.

The streetlights spread a faint bloom over the sidewalk, and Sammy and I passed through it, our galoshes squeaking on the snow. He had turned up the collar of his overcoat, so I couldn't see his face, only the smooth crown of his head. His tools — scissors, combs, clippers — rattled about in the black leather satchel he carried. For years, in his barber chair, I had felt his strong hands tipping my head forward so he could shave the wispy hairs from my neck, twisting me this way and that so he could clip and shear. "Where does the crow light?" he used to say to me when I was younger. "There," he would say, and slap his hand down on my leg with a force that would leave the red print of his fingers on my skin.

"That is a dandy song, isn't it, Perry?" His breath hung in the air, and I could taste the sharp metal of the cold. "That's a song about a poor sap who loses his girl to an old friend. A beautiful song. That's the kind of song a man should sing to a good woman."

Over the years, he had made something of a name for himself singing at weddings in small towns across the county. It wasn't uncommon to see young brides-to-be entering his shop to engage his service. His talent, and its appreciation, had given him a confidence I envied and feared.

"Do you sing, Perry?" He stopped beneath a street light and turned to me. He smelled of talcum powder and hair oil.

"No, sir. My mother said I didn't inherit her talent."

"I suppose that would be right." Sammy narrowed his eyes and studied me. "I don't see any fire in you. You seem sort of lukewarm. No, I don't imagine you'd be the kind to carry much of a voice."

At the chapel, my father put his hand on Sammy's back, between his shoulder blades, and escorted him into the embalming room. My father's hands were pallid, the grayish white of surgical gloves. They were small and unimpressive. Still, he was always using them to touch people: a slight pressure on a wrist, in the small of the back, nudging them in the direction he wanted them to go.

Twice a month, he and Sammy the Egg played war games in our basement. On a six-by-nine-foot board they reenacted Civil War battles, maneuvering miniature soldiers across valleys and rivers and bluffs. My father spent hour after hour painting each soldier, each musket and cannon, each stone wall. I liked to watch him tracing the fine hairs of his brush along cheekbones and jaw lines. That night, when he had left Sammy to his work, we sat together in the quiet of the basement, just outside the embalming room, and I admired the patience and the steady nerve it took for him to paint each figure.

He had taught me details he had acquired over years of study, and while Sammy cut Mr. Pettyjohn's hair, my father ambushed me with a quiz.

"What was the basic infantry weapon, Colonel?"

"The single-shot Springfield."

"Range?"

"Kill a man at half a mile."

"Outstanding. And the land mines, Colonel. What were they called in those days?"

"Booby traps."

"No. Concentrate. That was later. Then they called them 'infernal machines.'"

He told me how the Union divided the Confederacy by controlling the Mississippi, how they blockaded the coast, how Sherman broke the South on his march to the sea. "Anything he could use, he took. Everything else, he burned. The man was ruthless, a devil. 'War is hell,' he said. Your great-grandfather was along on that campaign. Imagine, Colonel. Your own flesh and blood."

When my father spoke to me of flanks and defense lines, artillery and ironclads, his voice exploded into a deep-chested song, a Gatling gun of joy. McClellan's goof at Sharpsburg, he said, was he didn't attack quickly enough. "He knew the Confederate army was divided, Colonel. He knew part of it had gone with Jackson to capture Harpers Ferry. Lee was vulnerable, only 50,000 men. McClellan had 87,000, but he waited."

"No fighting instinct," I said. "A popcorn fart in a mouse's ass."

"That's right. And what about Burnside? What was his mistake in the drive toward Richmond in '62?"

"He crossed the Rappahannock at Fredricksburg."

"Go on."

"It was the strongest point in the Confederate line. Lee massacred him."

"Bingo. Remember, Colonel. Always hit a man at his weakest spot."

That winter, my father's zest for these maneuvers had snared me. I had fallen in love with the strategy of war, with the use of cunning and pluck. Nights, while pupils played "Heart and Soul" on my mother's piano, my father and I bowed our heads over topographical maps. Together we aligned our regiments, and together we planned our attacks.

And that particular night, I could hear Sammy the Egg at work in the embalming room: the snip-snip-snip of his scissors, his baritone voice. "Yes, sir," he said. "Indeed sir." As if Mr. Pettyjohn had just offered an opinion on politics or the weather. "That's right, sir. Oh, yes, sir. You are one hundred percent hunky-dory correct about that."

The nights of wakes, Sammy would linger by the casket, eavesdropping on the mourners as they commented on the deceased's appearance. From time to time, someone would mistake him for one of the survivors. "No, sir," he would say whenever they would shake his hand and offer their condolences. "I'm not family. I just do the hair."

My father had long despised Sammy's lack of respect for the rites of death and had been casting about for another barber, one who would better revere the solemn rituals my father himself had come to admire. He had settled on Loyal Hall, a Presbyterian from Bridgeport who wore bow ties and swept his floor after every haircut.

"Loyal Hall keeps a clean shop," my father said as he listened to Sammy chattering away in the embalming room. "And he doesn't fill your ear with jibber-jabber. The next time I need someone, he's the man."

Sammy started whistling "Pop Goes the Weasel," and when I heard him, I laughed.

My father laid down his paint brush. "Perry, mourners expect a professional, considerate demeanor." He drew back his shoulders. "Never smile. Even if you mean it as a kindness, it will always come out wrong. Keep yourself under control, and never — do you understand? — never let it show that you feel someone's pain."

Sammy came from the embalming room, fastening the gold clasp on his leather satchel. "Well, that's done," he said. "Another satisfied customer. That's what I like about this job. No complaints. Hey, Roy? It's like they say about you undertakers. You're lucky. You can bury your mistakes."

My father stood and shook Sammy's hand. "Thank you for coming," he said. "Particularly at this late hour."

"Is it late?" Sammy looked at his wristwatch. "So it is. I was hoping to have a word with your missus."

"Lois?" My father said her name with a dead tongue as if he hadn't said it in a long time.

"That's right," said Sammy. "I'll only be a minute. Don't worry, Roy. I won't steal her."

We watched Sammy climb the stairs, and only when I heard him on the next flight that led to our living quarters, did I say to my father, "Why didn't you tell him about Loyal Hall?"

"Patience, Colonel," my father said. "Surrender is always a delicate matter. If it's to be accepted, it requires the proper time and atmosphere. Now, about tomorrow's battle."

We were discussing our strategy for Gettysburg, when we heard my mother's shrill cry, as if in panic or alarm, and we raced up the stairs, my father leading the way.

My mother and Sammy the Egg were sitting at the kitchen table, having a glass of beer. They were laughing, and when my mother threw up her hands and tossed back her head, I thought of the girls at school — pretty and capable of spooking timid boys like me with their looks. It fascinated me to see the girl my mother had once been in her eyes, in the blush coloring her cheeks, in the way she bit her lip when she noticed my father and me standing in the archway, watching her.

"Holy cow," she said. "Where's the fire?"

My father was panting for breath. He bent over, his hands on his knees. "I heard you scream," he said.

"That's a hoot." My mother tapped Sammy on the arm. "Isn't that a riot?"

"I just told her a joke," Sammy said. "Pull back the troops, Roy. We were just having a chuckle."

My father straightened. He ran his hand over his head, mussing his hair. I thought how silly we looked, the two of us, and I tried to justify our charge up the stairs. "I heard it, too," I said. "I thought something was wrong."

"We were just shooting the breeze," my mother said. "Sammy was telling me about his nephew."

"My sister's kid," said Sammy. "Joey Scarbo. He's coming to live with me. Be here tomorrow. His old man died in Korea, and now the kid needs a little direction. You know how it is with kids. Wild hairs."

My mother shrieked again. She slapped her hand against Sammy's shoulder. "Wild hairs," she said. "That's a scream. Uncle Sammy — *Il Barbiere di Siviglia* — he's going to take care of those wild hairs." She took a long drink of her beer. "Wild hairs," she said again. "Get it, Roy?"

"I got it," said my father.

"Lois is going to give the kid piano lessons." Sammy smiled. "We'll see if he's got any of my musical talent."

"At ease, boys." My mother raised her hand to her forehead and snapped off a salute. "Go back to whatever it was you were doing. We're shipshape here. Eh, Sammy? Believe me, Roy. Everything is A-okay."

LATE THAT night I woke, shivering and cold. My mother had come into my room and opened my window, and the icy air was sweeping across my bed.

"Perry, come here." She was standing by the window, and the curtains were lifting and falling around her. "I want to tell you something."

Her voice was pleasant and inviting, and I couldn't help but go to it.

She pointed out the window to the sky where stars were bright above the rooftops and the trees. "A long time ago, Perry, people believed that each of the planets made a distinct musical note while it was spinning. The music of the spheres, they called it, even though no one had ever heard it. It was too majestic, they swore, to ever be heard by human ears." I could smell the warm flannel of her nightgown and a scent of roses her bath salts had left on her skin. "Do you think it's the same with our spirits, Perry? Do you think when we die, our souls spin off into space, and for eternity they make a grand music no one on earth can hear — a music so rare and dear it's not to be had for love?"

My mother, in those days, could frighten me with her passion for mysteries I felt certain would be forever closed to my ordinary imagination. "Mr. Pettyjohn's gone, Perry." She put her arms around me and pulled me close to her. "And here we are. And what can we hear?"

"Your heart."

"Good. That's music. Percussion."

"No," I told her. "It's complete systoles and diastoles. It's the heart's chambers emptying and then filling with blood. That's what stopped when Mr. Pettyjohn died."

"I know where you learned *that*." She let me go and slammed the window shut. "It chills me, Perry — honestly, it does — to see what your father's done to you."

THE NEXT morning at breakfast, my father said, "I've got a joke."

My mother looked at him as if he were someone she had never seen. She looked at him as if he were someone interesting, someone she would like to get to know.

"A joke, Roy?" she said.

"That's right. Something amusing I heard last month at that funeral directors' conference. Just let me think a minute." He cocked his head to the side and put his finger to his lips. "Okay," he said. "I've got it. Listen to this: 'What did the corpse say to the mortician?' "

I saw my mother's spine stiffen; her shoulders went back, and her chin lifted. For a long time, no one said anything. Then, finally, I couldn't take it anymore, and I said, "What? What did the corpse say to the mortician?"

My father started to giggle. " 'Make it high octane. Lately, I've been running a little sluggish.' "

My mother pushed her chair back from the table.

"No, wait," my father said. "That's not right. 'What did Henry Ford say to the mortician?' Get it? Henry Ford? High octane?"

"I think that's in bad taste," my mother said. "I don't think that's funny at all."

THAT AFTERNOON, Sammy the Egg came to recreate Gettysburg. His nephew, Joey, was with him. He was a tall boy with wavy hair cut in a ducktail, and he was wearing motorcycle boots, a pair of Levis slung low on his slim hips, and a red satin jacket whose back was emblazoned with fire-breathing dragons coiled around a map of Korea.

"Who's this?" My father was wearing his Union Cavalry Commander hat, the front of the blue felt laced with crossed sabers, and he brought the brim down closer to his eyes as if Joey were a Confederate spy threatening to ferret out some piece of strategy. "Reinforcements, Sammy?"

"My nephew." Sammy put a hand on Joey's back and shoved him forward until he and my father were nearly nose to nose. "Look at that hair. You'd think he was one of those doo-wop boys. Some day I'll get him in the chair. A nice crew cut, I figure. Maybe a burr."

When Joey moved, his satin jacket rustled and hissed. "Joseph Scarbo," he said, offering his hand to my father. "What were you in, Mr. Sievers? World War II, I figure. What was it? North Africa? Normandy? The Philippines?"

"Asthma," said Sammy. "A medical deferment. Right, Roy?"

My father nodded, and it was clear to me, in a way it had never been, that Sammy the Egg knew too much. "You cut enough hair," he had told me once, "you hear enough stories. You get a knack for seeing people for what they are. Secrets? Forget it. A snip here, a snip there, and I get down to the scalp. I can tell you, friend, things about yourself you forgot you even knew."

Sammy, as always, played the Confederacy. My father, from the beginning, had insisted on playing the Union, and Sammy had accepted his own role as Johnny Reb, bowing to his host with Southern grace and charm.

Nothing rattled Sammy. His thick legs kept him anchored, and his bald head and grin reminded me of one of those roly-poly dolls, those inflatable clowns that always came back to you, no matter how hard you punched them. On this day, he positioned his brigades on the perimeter of Cemetery Hill, from Devil's Den to Seminary Ridge, and along my father's right flank at Culp's Hill. It was the strategy Lee had employed in 1863, and it surprised my father since Sammy rarely followed the course history had set. "It didn't work then," he always said. "Why the hell would it work now?"

His moves were often haphazard and stunning, glorious and devil-may-care, and over the winter he had captured me with the charm of his backasswards bravado. Still, the allegiance I felt myself give to him disturbed me because I could see, beneath his good-natured bluster, that he was a cruel man who enjoyed destroying my father's austere and arrogant confidence in history.

Sammy unbuttoned his cuffs and rolled his sleeves back over his arms. "Kid," he said to Joey. "I'm going to show these blue-coats a thing or two. Why don't you go upstairs and introduce yourself to Lois. You'll know her when you see her. She's the only one in this joint who's got any life."

"You're the general," said Joey. "I'm just along for the ride."

For once, my father and I had decided to depart from the facts of the battle. Instead of positioning our main line along the left wing, as General Meade had done, we had shifted our power to the right, anticipating Sammy's probable attack at Culp's Hill. "Pickett charged the left flank at Seminary Ridge," my father had said the night before, when we had finalized our strategy. "Straight into Meade's force. They could have turned the right flank at Culp's Hill, but they didn't. Why not, Colonel?"

"No cavalry reconnaissance. They never knew how much they had weakened that part of the Union line."

"Good report, Colonel. You know Samuel will try to pull his usual stunt. This time, we'll be ready."

But we weren't. There he was, the bulk of his troops entrenched along Seminary Ridge, waiting for the proper roll of the dice to permit his charge across the Great Wheat Field Farm, in a position, as Pickett had never been, to capture Cemetery Hill.

"That's a travesty," my father said.

"That's war," said Sammy the Egg. He rubbed his hands together. "Strike up the drums. Sound the charge. Let's shoot dice."

It didn't take long for Cemetery Hill to fall to Sammy's troops. "Look at that," he said when it was over. "I'll be damned, Roy. We just rewrote history."

My father grabbed onto the edge of the game board and bowed his head. Sammy took a set of car keys from his pocket and handed them to me. "Be a sport, and take these to Joey," he said. "Tell him I'm going to walk home. Tell him he can try out the Oldsmobile. Go along with him, Perry. Show him the sights. Would that be all right, Roy? Part of the terms of surrender?"

My father raised his head. "Fine," he said. "All spoils to the victor. Whatever you say."

UPSTAIRS, my mother was sitting beside Joey on the piano bench. Her fingers were long and slender, and they trembled as she held them arched above the keys. I could see in the flared wings of her shoulder blades and the delicate sweep of her back, the lovely girl she had been when she had first met my father.

"This is a C-major scale," she said to Joey. "Now watch me." Each note sounded pure and clear in the still room, and I stood, half-hidden in the doorway, listening to my mother. "C, D, E — thumb under — F, G, A, B, C. And then back. See? Easy as pie."

If I closed my eyes, I could conjure up the sound of her singing at funerals, her soprano rising sweet and pure from the rear of the chapel. I could see her as a young bride, alone in her bedroom: laying out my father's suit, brushing lint from his jacket, choosing his necktie, buffing his shoes. But it all embarrassed me, this intimate glimpse into the life they had once had, a life that had ended when my mother had grown weary of the somber climate which had become the due course of their days together.

"My husband Roy made a rhyme once to match up with the notes," she told Joey. She played the scale again. "Pretty is as pretty does, my lovely Lois always was." She laughed, and then quickly covered her mouth with her hand. "Goodness, I haven't thought of that in years."

"That's funny," Joey said. "An undertaker who writes rhymes."

"You wouldn't think it to know him now," my mother said. "But he used to have pizazz. Do you know what his favorite radio program was? 'The Fleishman Hour' with Rudy Vallee. Bob Hope was on that show, and his catch phrase was 'Who's Yehoodi?' I don't remember what he meant by it, but Roy loved it. He used to sneak up behind me, put his hands over my eyes, and say it. 'Who's Yehoodi?' he used to say, and I'd let my head fall back against his chest, and I'd whisper, 'Heigh-ho, everybody' — that's what Rudy Vallee always said, you see — 'You are,' I'd say. 'You, Roy. You're my hoodi.' "

My mother wound the metronome on the piano and set it to ticking. "Well, that's a silly story," she said. "That's all that is. Just forget it. Sometimes my mouth just runs and runs, and I can't shut up." She grabbed the metronome's pendulum, and the room went still. "I don't have many friends. I lost one of them yesterday. It's not that people don't like me; they just don't think about getting to know an undertaker's wife."

"It's sort of creepy," Joey said. "This whole place. Stiffs all around. But it's sort of cool, too. I bet you've got stories."

My mother grabbed Joey by the arm and pulled him up from the piano bench. "I want you to hear something," she said. Before she could lead him out into the hallway, I retreated a few steps down the stairs, afraid that they would see me. But they didn't. I heard my mother pick up the telephone and dial a number. "Listen," she said.

I counted to ten, trying to decide whether I should come out of hiding. Then I heard Joey say, "It's 2:25, thirty-two degrees."

"That's me," my mother told him.

"You?"

I imagined my father downstairs in the chapel, leaning over Mr. Pettyjohn's casket. He might be using a cotton swab and some rouge to liven up Mr. Pettyjohn's cheeks, last minute details now that he had the body in the chapel's light. I couldn't shake from my head the sight of him prancing to my mother, surprising her with his call — "Who's Yehoodi?" — and I began to grieve for such joy they had lost. What's more, I began to fear the life I would one day inherit.

I heard Joey lay the telephone receiver back in its cradle, and I came up the stairs.

"Perry," my mother said. "You little mouse. You crept right up on us."

"Sammy sent me up here to give these to Joey." I held up the car keys. "He said we should go for a ride so I can show him the sights."

"Yes," my mother said. "You two should scoot. Joey's spent long enough listening to this crazy old dame. Go on. The both of you. Get some fresh air. Enjoy what's left of the day."

DOWNSTAIRS, in the foyer, Joey jerked his thumb toward the chapel doors. "Is that where you have the funerals?"

"That's right," I said. "We have a visitation this evening. Mr. Pettyjohn." I could hear my father moving about in the basement, and my mother upstairs turning on the radio. "I'll give you a look," I said. "Come on."

My father had dressed Mr. Pettyjohn in the gray suit Mrs. Pettyjohn had brought for him. I could see that much when Joey and I stepped into the chapel, that and Mr. Pettyjohn's eyeglasses and the tip of his nose just visible over the edge of the mahogany casket.

Joey's boots clomped over the polished floor. We stood at Mr. Pettyjohn's casket as if we were any two mourners, paying our respects.

"Just like the frogs in biology class," Joey said. "Pickled in formaldehyde."

"Actually it's a mixture," I said, in a voice I hoped would impress Joey with my knowledge. "Formaldehyde, glycerin, borax, phenol, alcohol, and water. That's what does the trick. Most people don't know that."

Joey lifted an eyebrow. "Okay, smart guy, you know what the twilight zone is?"

It would be a few years before the Rod Serling television show of that name, and I said, no, I didn't.

"It's the lowest level of the ocean light can still reach. One more inch and you're in darkness forever. How about that? You probably thought I was a dummy, but I'm not."

I lifted Mr. Pettyjohn's hand. "Touch it," I said. "Here." I stroked my finger over the tendons that led down from the knuckles to the wrist. "You can feel where we injected cream to fill in the sunken spots."

"I don't want to touch it," Joey said. "I want that ring." He pointed to Mr. Pettyjohn's wedding band. "You're the expert here. Go on, Dr. Death. Take it off."

At that instant, a brief and dazzling moment that seized me, I fell in love with Joey, with the danger of him. I twisted the wedding band free.

"This is because we can," Joey said. "This is risk, pure and simple. That's how you know your ticker's still kicking. Meanness and ruin. That's what trips my trigger. Shout hallelujah, Perry. Jesus yes. Shits-ka-tits. Amen."

I laid Mr. Pettyjohn's left hand back over his right, taking care to leave them in that pose my father called the "at ease" posture. I could imagine him working over a corpse, forcing a limb seized with rigor mortis into a position that satisfied him, and it seemed to me a lonely and sorrowful thing to spend your life doing.

I'll say it again: I loved Joey Scarbo, loved him because he made me feel criminal, made me drunk with the joy of unbridled risk.

"Ring-a-ding-ding," he said. "Let's scram."

We escaped the still of the chapel, suffocating with its overwhelming scent of gladiolus and snapdragons and mums, and rode in Sammy's Olds 88 out the blacktop, deep into the country.

Joey steered with one finger laid across the lower rim of the wheel, as if he needed no more than that to feel the grade and roll of the road unwinding beneath us. He bumped the 88 through its gears, punched the accelerator, shoved at the limits of caution and good sense until the countryside was flashing by, and I could feel in my stomach the dip of each hill, the lean of every curve. I was no longer Perry Sievers, the undertaker's son, straight-faced and sober in his Robert Hall suit; I had spun loose from myself, lost all center and gravity, and for that terrible and frightening freedom I gave thanks.

"This is for Pettyjohn," Joey said. "This is for all the dead everywhere."

He slipped the ring over his thumb and held his hand, fingers splayed, up for my approval. "We'll keep it until this guy's wife has sunk to her lowest point — twilight zone time — then we'll put it in an envelope and leave it in her mailbox. A gift from the dead. Special delivery. Won't she be surprised?"

I remembered the afternoons the Pettyjohns had come to our home to listen to the opera. They had been my mother's friends when too many others in our town had avoided her. Mrs. Pettyjohn, despite her stern manner in the classroom, was a goodhearted woman who believed in love, and I didn't want her to have the shock of opening Joey's envelope and seeing Mr. Pettyjohn's wedding band.

I said, "It's lousy what we've done. Give me the ring."

Joey pulled the 88 off the blacktop and sat there while it idled, tapping the ring against the steering wheel. Gusts of wind swept in from the north and rocked us. I watched the low clouds banking in the west, the sky the color of lead, and I knew we would have snow by nightfall.

"It hurts me that you should say that," Joey said. "I thought we were going to be friends."

His voice — low and sharp — a suture needle piercing skin, razored me. In any war game, my father had told me, there were a limited number of moves, and each one eliminated another. "If you get in a tight spot," he had explained. "All you can hope for is some piece of business so bold, so unexpected, you turn your fortune around."

I had fallen in with Joey and had become a thief. At that moment, I could feel my life surrounding me, my opportunities for escape dwindling. The way I figured it, I could continue to close rank with Joey and keep mum about Mr. Pettyjohn's wedding band, or I could come clean, and surrender myself to my father.

I reached over and snatched the ring from Joey's thumb. "No," I said. "We can't be friends."

I didn't know what sort of life I wanted, but I knew I didn't want Joey's life, a lowdown life full of mean-spirited intentions and underhanded tactics. I was scared because I didn't know what was going to happen next, but all he did was tell me the story of the day he found out his father was dead.

What troubled him most was the fact that he couldn't cry. "Zippo," he said. "Not a tear. I thought I was a heartless bastard. Then a few days after the funeral, a package came. You know, one of those boxes wrapped in brown paper and tied with string. It was this jacket the old man had sent me from Korea. I kept seeing him on leave, picking it out for me, folding it just so, and putting it in that box. I kept seeing him tying that string — one of the last things he would ever do — tying it tight so that package would make it across the ocean to me, and I broke down. Don't laugh. You see, I wasn't a heartless bastard after all. I'm not ashamed to tell you about it. Me, Joseph Scarbo. Swear to God. I bawled like a baby. For a minute, my old man was alive again. Let me tell you, I thank St. Christopher and the Blessed Virgin Mary that box came."

I kept staring at the cloud banks rolling in from the west. Already, sleet was spraying the windshield with its fine shot. I remembered what my father had taught me about never showing I felt someone else's pain. I closed my hand around Mr. Petty-john's wedding band.

"You don't get it, do you?" Joey said. "Don't you see I'm the good guy here?" He raced the 88's motor, cranked the wheel, and spilled us out onto the blacktop, tires screaming, singeing the air with the smell of hot rubber. "If you ask me, you're the lousy son-of-a-bitch. I want to bring back the dead. All you want to do is bury them."

The 88 dipped into an S-curve, and I closed my eyes. I braced myself for the lean and twist, waited for the violent shift I trusted to sling us free.

THAT NIGHT, our telephone rang. My mother was playing "Mona Lisa" on the piano, and she held a chord and then let it go. "It's bad news," she said. "I know it."

My father came upstairs, rolling down his shirt sleeves.

"This one will be felt," he said. "My, yes. Most unfortunate. A young boy."

"A boy?" My mother closed the keyboard cover.

"Joey Scarbo. Sammy's nephew. Such a shame. Snap to, Colonel."

I was sitting on the piano bench next to my mother, and I recalled the moment I had seen her sitting there beside Joey, playing scales, her trembling fingers reaching for the next note, each building on the last. It hit me, then, that she must have loved Joey for his timely entrance into her life, as if he had been sent to her to replace the friend she had lost when Mr. Pettyjohn had died.

"It's a horrible thing," she said to me. "A horrible, horrible thing." She closed her hand around my arm. "You know that, don't you, Perry? What a tragedy this is?"

The clock on the piano chimed eleven. My father tightened the knot in his necktie.

"Colonel?"

"Yes, sir."

"It's time we got started."

Although it sounds terrible to say it now, the truth is I felt a tremendous freedom, knowing Joey was dead. I felt as if someone had given my life back to me, and I wanted to tell my mother not to worry. I was going to be all right. But then she stood up from the piano bench, and she clutched her robe closed at her throat. "Go on," she said to me, and her voice was ugly and raw. "Go," she said again. "Go be his little Nazi."

I DROVE the hearse with care. The streets were slick with snow, and the tire chains rattled and clanked.

"Imagine, Perry," my father said. "Joey. A boy your age."

Joey had smashed Sammy's 88 on the S-curve, had clipped a bridge abutment. I imagined the 88 hurled into space, spinning an uncommon trajectory, something wild which held no claim to earth.

"Keep both hands on the wheel," my father told me. "Up high where everyone can see them. If they can see your hands, they'll know you're a square Joe. They'll know you've got everything under control."

At the Texaco, the 88 hung from the wrecker's winch. Boys with their jacket collars turned up, their shoulders hunched against the wind, circled the car. They tapped a wheel with their boots, they squatted on their haunches to see how the fenders had peeled back, how the motor had shoved itself through the fire wall.

Farther away, at a safe distance, girls wrapped their arms around their chests and stamped their feet in the snow.

When the hearse's headlights swept over them, the girls

stopped shuffling their feet, the boys straightened and lifted their faces. They stared at us — the girls with their bobby sox drooping from their calves, the boys with their hands shoved into their jacket pockets, everyone's face red from the cold.

"Don't look at them, Colonel," my father said. "Come to attention."

"Sir?"

"Eyes straight ahead. Don't embarrass them. Don't let them know how precious they are in their grief."

IT WAS after midnight when we eased the gurney, clacking along its rollers, out the back of the hearse. Joey's weight came to us, shifting and settling in the body bag. I could feel it in my arms, and suddenly the loose rattle of muscles and organs and bones undid me, and I said to my father, "I stole Mr. Pettyjohn's wedding band. I've got it here in my suit jacket. I know it was a wicked thing to do."

My father lifted his face to the second-story window where my mother's piano lamp cast a faint and distant glow. "Better classify that information, Colonel," he said to me. "Wouldn't want it to fall into enemy hands." He put a finger to his lips. "Top secret. Better keep it on the qt."

THE NEXT morning Sammy the Egg came to make Joey's funeral arrangements.

"Shouldn't we wait for your sister?" my father said.

Sammy thumped his fist against his chest. "I'm the one responsible here."

I had stayed home from school for Mr. Pettyjohn's funeral later that morning, and I was standing with Sammy and my father in the foyer, just outside the chapel. Sammy was clutching his black leather satchel. It was a frigid day, and he had brought in the smell of the cold and the damp. It was a gamy, rotten smell, and when I looked at him — the way he stood with his head bowed, the shiny egg of his skull raw and gleaming in the light — I could see how close he was to coming apart.

"And another thing." He gave the satchel a shake, and I heard the combs and clippers and scissors clank together. "I want to cut the hair."

My father shook his head. "That wouldn't be decent. You being family. No, I couldn't let you do that."

"I've got a right to do this," Sammy said. "Listen, Roy. No one else should cut that boy's hair."

"No," my father said. "That's one thing I absolutely won't allow. I'll get Loyal Hall. He'll do a good job."

Sammy's shoulders dropped; his chest fell. "Loyal Hall," he said. "Jesus Christ." He let loose a great sigh as if all the air were leaving him. He rocked back on his heels, and I had to catch him to keep him from falling. As he leaned into me, I staggered with his weight.

"Steady," my father said, coming to my rescue. "Easy now. It's all right, Perry. I've got him." The two of us ushered Sammy into the grief counseling room. We slipped off his coat and eased him into a chair.

"I promised my sister I'd look out for that kid," he said. "Make him toe the line, put him into shape."

"Tell your mother we'd like some coffee," my father said to me.

"How do you like your coffee, Sammy? Black? Make it black, Perry."

"Black it is," I said.

Upstairs, my mother was having her own coffee at the kitchen table. She was still in her bathrobe, and her hair was in curlers for Mr. Pettyjohn's funeral. She was stirring sugar into her coffee, her hand making lazy circles, the spoon clinking against the cup. We hadn't spoken since the night before when she had called me my father's little Nazi, and for a moment I hesitated, afraid to approach her.

I watched her idly stirring her coffee. I knew she had tried her best to sweeten her days there above the chapel. She had listened to opera with the Pettyjohns on Saturday afternoons, she had given piano lessons, and once Sammy the Egg had told her a joke — a corny joke: "What's black and white and red all over?" — and she had been so lonely she had howled, nearly screamed with thanksgiving.

And I loved her for her loneliness, but I couldn't tell her that, because I was sixteen and I didn't know how to tell my mother I felt sorry for her. So I tapped my knuckles against the archway, and she lifted her head.

"Perry." It startled me to hear her say my name. "Did I hear someone come in downstairs? Was it Mrs. Pettyjohn?"

"No, it was Sammy. Dad sent me up to get him some coffee."

"For Sammy?" She patted the curlers in her hair. "Poor Sammy. I'll get dressed. Tell your father I'll bring that coffee down in just a jiff."

FROM THE top of the stairs, I could see below me the toes of the overshoes — women's overshoes — barely visible, as if their owner had tried to hide herself and hadn't done an adequate job. They were Mrs. Pettyjohn's overshoes; I could see that as I came farther down the stairs. She was standing with her head bowed, her pocketbook hanging from her arm, an embroidered handkerchief twisted in her hand. She was wearing a cloth coat and a black hat with a net veil over her eyes.

"I didn't want to disturb anyone." Snow was melting from her boots, pooling up on the carpet. She tapped her heels together. "Oh, my. Look what a mess I'm making. It is a mess, isn't it, Perry? And I didn't want to be any bother."

"A little snow," I said, trying to keep my voice airy, but not exaggerated. "Let's get those overshoes off so you'll be more comfortable."

I took her elbow and helped her to a settee against the wall.

"I know it's early," she said. "But I thought if I came, I could have some time with him. You know what I'm saying, Perry. Some more time. Before the funeral."

She lifted each foot so I could unzip her overshoes and tug them free. One of her slippers came off, and she crossed her legs and pointed her toes so I could ease it back on.

All the while, I kept thinking how commanding she was in the classroom, her pointer whacking against the chalkboard as she marched us through our drills.

"Is it all right I came?" she asked me.

I held her hand and lifted her to her feet. "Let me help you with your coat," I said, "and then you can go on in."

IN THE GRIEF counseling room, Sammy the Egg was telling a story about my father.

"This was when we were kids, Perry. About the age you are now. I bet you don't even remember it, Roy. Me? I've kicked it over and over. I can't even look at you now without calling it to mind."

My father sat on the edge of the sofa, his knees together, his hands folded in his lap. "I don't know what you're talking about," he said. "Honestly, I don't have a clue."

"It was when my old man died. You were a pallbearer."

"Yes, I remember there weren't enough. I remember my father and I filled in. It was my first time."

"My old man was a drunk, Perry. That's the truth of it. I can't deny it. He was a drunk, and he didn't have enough friends to carry him to the grave. I was ashamed — I don't mind saying it. All I wanted was to get beyond that day, to get out of that graveyard and go on with my life, but then you did what you did, Roy. And now you don't even remember it, do you?"

My father shook his head. "That's ancient history."

"Not to me. I remember like it was yesterday. You took my hand. Not the way a man would — to shake it — but the way a girl would — to hold it. A sappy move like that, something you must have seen in the movies, and all I could do was stand there and let you do it."

I could hear, in his voice, the disgust Sammy had preserved and carried with him since that moment in the cemetery. I wanted to tell him I felt sorry for him, now that death had left him out in the open again, but then my mother opened the door and stepped into the room.

"Roy," she said, and my father looked up at her.

"Yes." His voice was faint, reaching out to her from the

small space Sammy had backed him into with his story. "I'm here."

They spoke in muted tones, their words half-whispered, a code only people who have loved each other a long time can use.

My mother pointed to the foyer. "Please."

"A problem?"

"Mrs. Pettyjohn."

"Yes?"

"A wedding band."

MR. PETTYJOHN 's ring was still in the breast pocket of my suit jacket. I had confessed my crime to my father. He had told me to keep it secret, and I had obeyed him.

"Do you know what it was like when your old man did that?" Sammy said to me after my mother and father had left the grief counseling room. "When he took my hand? That knucklehead. He was this kid with asthma, this kid no one gave a rat's ass for, and there he was holding my hand like he was Florence-fucking-Nightingale. Do you know what that was like?"

I suspected I did, but I wouldn't tell Sammy that. I wouldn't tell him because I didn't want him to know how my mother made me feel — "delicate" — as if I would never survive anything ugly or brutal in the world.

"It was like nothing I can tell you. It was like he could have done anything he wanted to me, and I would have let him. He blindsided me, and somehow I knew — even a dope like me — I knew how alone I was. So alone a boy like Roy Sievers could feel sorry for me, and I could let him."

I imagined my father, at my age, holding another boy's hand, and it gave me an odd and sickly feeling to know that I would have done the same thing. We were that much alike. I thought of how he used his hands to take people by the elbows — the slightest touch — to usher them into a car, to the guest register, to the gravesite. I thought of how I felt whenever I held the door open for mourners, when I carried flowers into the chapel, when I drove a car in a funeral procession, when I helped lower a casket into a grave. The only word I could think of to describe it was "love." As corny as it sounded, that's what it was, a deep and abiding love for all those left sweet and wanting: the women who clutched my hand as I helped them into their cars; the men who let me hold their coats for them and button them as if they were children; Sammy the Egg, who a few minutes before had crumpled against me. How easy it was to love them all, everyone who came to me mourning. That was my father's secret, the one he carried with him each time he presided over a death.

Outside in the foyer, Mrs. Pettyjohn's voice rose the way it did in class whenever someone mangled a verb conjugation. "For God's sake, Roy Sievers. Robbing the dead. You. A man we should all be able to trust."

The door to the grief counseling room flew open, and my father marched in.

"Get up," he said to Sammy, and Sammy, without a word, got to his feet.

My father's voice was low, the voice he used when he spoke to mourners, but now there was an edge to it, the sharpness he used when he barked out advances during war games. "I've had my eye on you," he said. He smoothed the lapels of Sammy's blazer with his small fingers. He buttoned the blazer and gave it a tug, stretching it tight across Sammy's shoulders. "You owe Mrs. Pettyjohn an apology, soldier."

My mother and Mrs. Pettyjohn had followed my father into the room. Mrs. Pettyjohn had balled her handkerchief up into her fist; my mother was holding her by the elbow, one arm across her shoulders.

"What is this?" Sammy said to my father. "What kind of crazy stunt are you trying to pull?"

"Tell him, Colonel," my father said, and I snapped to.

"Sir?"

"Tell him what we know."

I knew what my father wanted me to say, but Sammy was glaring at me. One look at his face and I could see that we were marching into dangerous territory. A few steps more and it would be too late. I knew I could save us — there was still that chance. All I had to do was tell the truth, confess that Joey and I had stolen the wedding band, take it from my pocket. But something held me back. I wanted to think that it was courage, that I was reckless and bold, but I knew it was only because I was a coward, afraid to betray my father.

Sammy was still staring at me, and I imagined something of what Joey must have felt — the horror — that moment in the S-curve when he must have known the 88 would never hold.

"He's been stealing from the corpses," I said. "Rings and stuff. That's what he's been doing."

Sammy's satchel was on the floor by his feet. "Maybe I

should check your bag," my father said. "See what you've got in here."

He leaned over to open the satchel, and Sammy jerked up his knee, catching my father in the face.

It was a quick and vicious blow, one that caught us by surprise, and I heard my mother say, "Roy." That was all. That one word — like a breath — and then my father was on his knees, holding his face in his hands, and Sammy was picking up the leather satchel and storming out the door, his shoulder knocking against me as he left.

Still holding onto Mrs. Pettyjohn, my mother again said, "Roy" — louder this time, as if she wanted him to know she was still there. Then she looked at me, and I had never seen such a helpless look on her face. I took Mrs. Pettyjohn and ushered her out into the foyer.

"It was his wedding band," Mrs. Pettyjohn said. "I didn't want to cause trouble, but I wanted him to have his wedding band. Now look what's happened."

Behind us, in the grief counseling room, my father was still on his knees. His shoulders were heaving, and my mother was kneeling beside him. She was trying to press him to her, as if he were someone lost and sweet, dear to her now in a way he had never been. Quietly, so as not to disturb them, I closed the door.

"Poor Perry," Mrs. Pettyjohn said. "The world must seem like a miserable place to you now. But don't worry. You're young. You'll survive all this. Remember, as long as one person knows *amo*."

"Yes, ma'am," I said, even though I was rotten with guilt.

Inside me, where my father had told me I would have to hollow out a space for other people's misfortune, my heart was ragged and worm-eaten.

Then I heard my parents' sobs, and they were like nothing I had ever heard. I stood in the foyer, their wails rising around me — my mother's, my father's — and I surrendered. I took it in, let it fill me up: their chorus of regret and desire, their grand artillery of grief.

# THE WELCOME TABLE

•　　•　　•　　•　　•　　•　　•　　•

THREE NIGHTS a week, when I was seventeen, my father took me downtown and made me shout "monkey," and "nigger," and "coon." He made me shout these things, he said, because he loved me. "Put your heart into it," he told me whenever my voice would falter. "Go on. Get with it. Give it everything you've got."

It was 1960, a touch-and-go time in Nashville. An activist named James Lawson was organizing students from the black colleges, and because my father sold greeting cards to black-owned variety stores, he had gotten word of the lunch counter sit-ins that were about to get underway. He had decided to hook up with the integration movement because he couldn't resist the drama of it. "This is history," he said to me one night. "The world is going to change, Ed, and someday you'll be able to say you were part of it."

He had volunteered my services as well because he knew I was at an age when it would be difficult for me to stand up for right, and he wanted me to get a head start on being a man of conscience and principle.

Our job was to prepare the students for the abuse they were sure to get. So, on those nights, in classrooms at Fisk University, we stood over the young men and women, and did our best to make their lives sad. My father was a handsome man with wavy hair and long, black eyelashes. He had a friendly smile and a winning way about him, but when he started his taunting, his face would go hard with loathing.

"Get the niggers," he would shout. "Let's get these monkeys out of here."

At his urging, I would join in. "Nigger," I would say, and my jaw and lips would tighten with the word.

We would pick at the students' hair. We would shove at them and pull them down to the floor.

When the workshop leader would call our demonstration to a halt, we would help the students up, and brush off their clothes, and laugh a bit, just to remind them that we were playacting. But always there would be heat in their eyes, because, of course, it was all different for them.

One of the students was a young man named Lester Bates. He had a reddish tint to his hair, and his hands were broad and long-fingered. One night, during a break, he clamped his hand around my wrist. I was holding a bottle of Coca-Cola, and he said to me, "Don't drop it. Hold on, boy. Keep a grip."

I could feel my hand going numb, my fingers tingling, and just when I was about to drop the bottle, Lester grabbed it. "This is going to get ugly," he said. "You know that, don't you? This whole town is going to explode." He took a drink from the bottle and handed it back to me. "Days like this make a body wonder what kind of stuff a man is made of."

He stood there, watching, and I did the only thing I could. I raised the bottle to my lips, and I drank.

I wanted to feel good about what we were doing — my father and I — but I hated him for bringing me into those classrooms. I hated him because he made my life uncomfortable. Some nights, on the way home, he would imagine a car was trailing us, and he would pull to the side of the street just to make sure we were safe. "There are limits," he said to me once, and he said it in a way that made it clear that he was one who knew those limits, and I was one who did not.

My father was Richard Thibodeaux, but it wasn't his real name. The previous spring, he had fled a scandal in New Hampshire. He had managed a cemetery there, and in the harsh winters, when the ground was so frozen graves were impossible to dig, the corpses were preserved in charnel houses until the spring thaw. Then, sometime in April, assembly-line burials began: the air shook with the raucous sound of heavy machinery digging the plots, the cranes hoisting concrete liner vaults from flatbed trucks. Sometimes, in the rush, the wrong bodies were put into the wrong graves, a fact that came out when one of the grave diggers spilled the news.

After that, we didn't stand a chance. It was a small town, and the rumors were vicious. We were cannibals, devil worshippers; we all had sex with corpses.

"How can we live here now?" my mother said one night to my father. "You've ruined us."

So we came south to Nashville. My mother, who had been there once to the Grand Ole Opry, chose it for its friendliness.

"Anywhere," said my father, "away from this snow and ice."

Any city, he must have been thinking, large enough to forget its dead.

Our first morning there, we left my mother in the motor court cabin we had rented, and went looking for a cemetery. "That mess in New Hampshire," my father said. "Let's put it behind us."

Nashville was brilliant with sunshine. My father put the top down on our Ford Fairlane 500, a '57 Skyliner with a retractable hardtop, and we drove past antebellum estates with guitarshaped swimming pools and manicured lawns landscaped with azalea bushes and dogwood trees. My father whistled a Frank Sinatra tune — "Young at Heart" — and for the first time since we had left New Hampshire, I believed in what we were doing.

"Don't think I'm a wicked person," my father said.

"I don't," I told him.

"People make mistakes, Ed." He lifted a hand and rubbed his eyes. "This must seem like a dream to you."

"It's something interesting," I said. "Something I might read about."

"That's you." He slapped me on the leg. "Steady Eddie. Just like your mother."

My mother was at a time in her life when her looks were leaving her, but instead of complaining, she had developed a habit of surrounding herself with beautiful things. In New

Hampshire, she had learned how to do eggshell art. She would take an egg and poke a hole in each end with a pin she had saved from an old corsage. Then she would insert the pin and break the yolk, hold the egg to her mouth, and blow out the insides. She would soak each eggshell in bleach, dry it, and then spray it with clear acrylic paint.

The paint strengthened the shell, and my mother could then use cuticle scissors to cut away a section: an oval, or heart-shaped, or teardrop opening into the hollow egg. Inside the shells, she painted background scenery, and then with plaster of paris, she built platforms on which she could position miniature figures, some of them only a quarter of an inch tall, to create scenes she would then name: "Chateau against Snow-Covered Mountains," "Collie Waiting by Stone Wall," "Skier Sliding down Icy Slope." It was a precise and painstaking art, each motion calculated and sure. The shells were surprisingly strong, and she rarely broke one. If one did happen to shatter, she would throw it away and start again. "Why curse your mistakes?" she said to me once. "Why not look at them as new opportunities?"

My father had come to Nashville, hoping for a new start at life, and that day in the cemetery, beneath the boughs of a cedar tree, he found what he was looking for: the headstone of a child who had died at the age of two in 1920, the year of my father's birth.

"That's going to be my name now," he said. "Richard Thibodeaux. It's a good southern name, don't you think?"

"What about your old name?" I asked him. "What about my name?"

He said he would go to the County Clerk's office and get a copy of Richard Thibodeaux's birth certificate. Then he would pay a visit to the Social Security Administration and apply for a card under his new name. If anyone got curious about why, at his age, he was just then getting around to applying for a card, he would tell them his parents had been Baptist missionaries, that he had been born in Tennessee, but had gone with his parents to South America where he had spent nearly all his adult life carrying out their work.

"What about me?" I said. "What's my story?"

My father put his finger to his lips and thought a moment. "That's a snap," he finally said. "I met your mother, the fair and pious daughter of a coffee plantation owner, an American from New Orleans, married her, and nine months later, you were born. You were a delicate child, given to fevers and ailments of the lungs. Finally, we had no choice but to send you back to America, away from the tropics, to live with your aunt in Memphis." He put his arms around me and pressed me to him. "And now here we are, united again. You see how easy it is? I'll tell anyone who gets nosy we're starting a new life."

And that's what he did. Once he had the birth certificate and the social security card, the rest was a breeze. We rented a modest home, and my father became Richard Thibodeaux, region five sales representative for the Glorious Days Greeting Card Company. He finagled some school forms from a print shop he knew and concocted a set of records for me. He gave me a near-perfect attendance record at Memphis East High School, excellent marks in citizenship, better grades than I had ever been able to manage.

"There," he said. "Now, you're set. A completely new profile. *Alacazam*."

He wanted to make sure no one ever linked our name with what he had begun to call "that misery in New Hampshire."

"I lost my self-respect there," he said to me. "That's the worst thing that can happen to a man."

My mother's eyes sparkled when she learned our new last name. "Penny Thibodeaux," she said, and I knew, like me, she had fallen in love with the elegant sound of those three syllables.

In school, when teachers called me by my full name — *Edward Thibodeaux* — I answered "yes, sir," or "yes, ma'am." I developed a soft-spoken gentility and impeccable manners. The change of climate, my father said, had done us a world of good.

It was a sweet time for us there in Nashville. Saturday evenings, we drove downtown to the Ryman Auditorium and took in the Opry. My father's favorite singer was Hawkshaw Hawkins. He was tall and lean, and he wore his cowboy hat cocked back on his head. My mother preferred Jan Howard because she was graceful and had a sweet smile. After the show, we would cruise down Broadway, the top down on our Skyliner. We would drive by the music and record shops, and sometimes my mother would slide over next to my father, and I would lay my head back and close my eyes and let the night air rush over my face and give thanks for Nashville and the second chance we had hit upon there.

"The Athens of the South," my father said once. "Milk and honey. Folks here know style when they see it."

Each day at noon, whenever he was on his route, he would find a public rest room where he could change his shirt.

"You can tell a man by his clothes," he explained to me. "A tidy man lives a tidy life."

He wore suspenders, and linen suits, and wingtip shoes he polished and buffed each night before going to bed. He had monogrammed handkerchiefs and ties. He carried a new leather briefcase full of sample cards, and when he swept into stationery shops and drugstores, he doffed his Panama hat, and said to the ladies behind the counters, "It's a glorious day for Glorious Days."

The Glorious Days Greeting Card Company specialized in sensitivity cards: genteel messages to commemorate birthdays, anniversaries, weddings. Selling them, my father said, made him feel he was contributing to the general celebration of living. He had been occupied too long with the burying of the dead, with mourning and grief.

"A gloomy Gus is a grumpy Gus," he said one day. "But that's all behind me now. Nothing but blue skies. Isn't that right, Ed? Hey, from here on, we're walking the sunny side of the street."

I KNOW my father didn't mean to make trouble for me, but of course, that was the way it all worked out. Some boys at school had seen the two of us going through the gates at Fisk University, and before long, the word was out that I was a "nigger lover."

One day, a boy named Dale Mink said a group was going downtown to stir up a ruckus. He was the center on our basketball team and an honor student. He had already won a scholarship to Vanderbilt. Even now, I don't think he was a thug; he was just caught up in the ugliness of those days. The way of life he had always known was changing, and he was afraid. "Those nigras think they can get away with this," he said to me. "You're either with us, or you're not."

The lunch counter sit-ins had been going on for over a week. Downtown, at Kress's, McClellans, Woolworth's, Walgreens, black students were occupying stools even though the tencent stores had chosen to close their counters rather than serve them.

My father came and went through these stores, selling Glorious Days greeting cards. Each evening, at dinner, he told us how the students sat there, studying for their classes. They were remarkable, he said — "as sober as judges" — the young men in dark suits with thin lapels and white shirts as bright as judgment day, the girls poised, as they unwound their head scarves and folded their duffle coats over the backs of their stools.

Sometimes, my father said, a waitress would call him back to the kitchen and set him up with a hamburger and a Coca-Cola, on account of she knew him as a man on the road who needed a hot lunch.

"You actually do that?" my mother said one night. "You sit there and eat while those poor kids do without?"

In those days, my father had a smugness about the new life he was inventing for us. He was so sure of the right direction we were taking, he had convinced himself that we deserved special liberties.

"I never thought," he told my mother. "Call me an idiot. Lord alive."

My mother was, by nature, a cheerful woman, and once we had left New Hampshire, she did her best to believe her life had been handed back to her. She worked part-time in an arts and crafts shop, and afternoons, when I came home from school, she asked me to help her with her eggshells. She sensed, better than my father, how brutal these times would become — how they would ruin people — and she was determined to maintain a certain beauty and delicacy in my life. She showed me how to transform a quail egg into a basket by cutting out the handle and adorning it with pearls and velvet ribbons. Together, we made eggs into cradles and lined them with lace.

This all seemed to me a terribly womanly thing to do, but slowly her optimism won me. When I watched her paint background scenes on the eggshells — amazed at how a few strokes could create trees, clouds, blades of grass — I fell in love with the way vast landscapes yielded to her slightest effort. When I was with her, I believed she could shrink anything that was difficult or immeasurable.

"Proportion," she told me. "That's the key. Making things fit."

Finally, she let me paint scenes of my own, and when I did, my fingers tingled with the delicacy of their motions. In New Hampshire, I had fallen into some trouble — vandalism, truancy, petty thievery — and I convinced myself that each gentle stroke I made was saving me from a life of violence and mayhem.

I rode downtown that day with Dale Mink. In Kress's, a gang of boys from the high school were prowling behind the students at the lunch counter. The boys' shirt collars were turned up, and their heel taps were clacking over the tile floor. Somewhere in the store, a radio was playing WSM. Later, I would learn that the station's call letters came from its original owner, The National

Life and Accident Insurance Company, whose motto was "We Shield Millions." But I didn't know that then. I only knew I was in a place I didn't want to be. I was there because things were getting hot for me at school — "nigger lover" — and like most people, I wanted my life to be easy and sweet.

The radio went off, and one of the boys stepped forward, closer to the students, and said in a low, steady voice, "Get your coon asses off those stools."

The students refused to turn their heads or let their shoulders slump with shame. I noticed, then, that one of the students was Lester Bates. He closed the book he had been reading and put his hands on the edge of the counter. The girl next to him turned her head just a fraction of an inch, and I could see her lips move. "This is it," she said.

The high school boys were squawking now: *nigger* this and *nigger* that. Some of them were jostling the students. Dale Mink elbowed me in the side. I knew he was waiting for me to join in the jeering. If there is one thing I would want people to understand, all these years later, it would be this: I didn't want to be Dale Mink, only something like him.

So I shouted, "Nigger."

I had done it hundreds of times with my father at training sessions.

"Nigger," I shouted, and I convinced myself it was only a word, that I was only one voice swallowed up by the voice of the mob.

But then the gang surged forward, and I saw Dale Mink latch onto Lester Bates. Dale jerked him backward, onto the floor, and soon I heard the dull thuds of punches and kicks finding cheek-bones and ribs.

I'M ASHAMED to think now of the fear I helped cause Lester Bates and those other young men and women. I have never been able to watch news films from those days, and until now, I have kept my part in them a secret.

When I got home that afternoon, my mother was waiting for me so we could finish an eggshell we had been working on that week. It was a dining room scene. We had lined the inside of the shell with wallpaper, and had built a table and four chairs from balsa wood. We had upholstered the chair seats with velvet ribbons and made a tablecloth from lace. My mother had brought home three miniature figures from the arts and crafts store: a man, a woman, and a young boy.

"Here's your father and me," she said. She put the miniature man and woman into adjacent chairs. Then she handed the miniature boy to me. "And here's you. Go on, Ed. Have a seat."

I didn't know where to put the boy who was supposed to be me. After the scene at Kress's, I didn't know where I belonged. I closed my hand around the figurine and felt it press into my palm.

"There was a fight at Kress's today," I said. "At the lunch counter. A bunch of boys from school went down there, and I went along. I said some things, and now I wish I hadn't."

My mother put her hand over my fist. "Don't let yourself get caught up in this," she said. "Listen to me. People have to live their lives the best they can. We've had too much trouble as it is."

"I can't forget it," I said. "How do you forget something terrible you've done?"

"You do whatever you have to do to get beyond it." My mother opened my fist and took the figurine and sat it in the chair whose back was turned to us. "There," she said. "It's cozy, isn't it? Inviting. Let's call this one, 'The Welcome Table.' "

"There's nothing on the table," I said. "We're not doing anything."

My mother thought a moment. "We're waiting."

"For what?"

"Who knows?" She snapped her fingers. "Hey, Buster Brown, get out of your shoe. The sky's the limit. For whatever's going to happen next."

BECAUSE my mother worked at the arts and crafts store, she had made some friends. One of them was a woman named Dix Gleason, and sometimes in the afternoons she would drop by for a visit. My mother was thrilled and worried on these occasions, happy for the company, but afraid her hospitality would fall short of Dix's approval. "You'd think she'd give a party notice," she said the first time Dix's car pulled up to our curb. "Heaven's sake. What do I have in the kitchen? Mercy, let's see. What can I whip up to suit Miss Dix?"

Dix Gleason was a loud woman who left lipstick stains on my mother's drinking glasses. She called me *Eddie* in a whiny voice like Topo Gigio, the mouse puppet on *The Ed Sullivan Show*, and she called my mother *Henny Penny*, a nickname I knew my mother despised.

"Like I was some hysterical old dame," she said to me once. "Honestly. The idea."

Some afternoons, Dix brought her husband, The Commodore.

Commodore Gleason was an accident reconstruction specialist for the highway patrol. He was intimate with the facts of crash and disaster. At accident scenes, he measured skid marks, gauged road conditions, interviewed survivors. He calculated the speed of travel, the angle of impact, reconstituted the moment of poor judgement or unfortunate circumstance.

"I can raise the dead," he boasted to us once after he had testified at a coroner's inquest. "I can bring them back to that moment where everything is A-okay. They're driving a Chevrolet down Route 45, just before eight p.m. The road is dry, visibility is fifteen miles, their speed is fifty-eight miles per hour."

If he could only leave them there, he said, happy and safe in their ignorance. But he knew too much. He knew that thirty miles up the road a Pontiac was streaking their way, that they would meet head-on at the top of a hill just before sunset.

"It's a burden to know as much as I do," he told us. "Take it from me: men are fools more often than not."

I was afraid of The Commodore. He had a way of making me feel nothing in my life would ever be safe.

Once, he came to my school and showed a blood-and-gore film about highway safety and traffic fatalities. He was snappy and regulation in his uniform: necktie firmly knotted, collar tips pointed, badge gleaming, trousers pressed, belt buckle polished. He told us about head-on crashes, decapitations, body bags.

"I know what you're thinking," he said. "You're thinking, this can't happen to me. That's what we all think. That's why we have to prepare ourselves for every hazard. Even you cool cats. Hell, you think you'll live forever."

One afternoon, my mother had sent me to the store for ice cream, and The Commodore had insisted we take his car. "You drive, sport," he said to me.

Before I could start the car, he jerked the keys from the ignition.

"Imagine the moment, Edward." He shook the keys in his hand as if they were dice. "That instant of horror when you know you're losing control. Your speed is too high, the road is too slick, the curve is too sharp. You're at that place you never dreamed you'd be. Brink of disaster, pal. One wrong move, and you cross over. Too late to get yourself back to safe ground. What do you do?"

"Don't panic," I said.

"And?"

"React."

He tossed me the keys. "Okay, Speedy Alkaseltzer. Let's see if you've got any pizz."

The afternoon my mother and I finished "The Welcome Table," our doorbell rang.

"Ding-dong," Dix Gleason shouted. "It's Dix and The Commodore."

The Commodore was off-duty. He was wearing a salt-and-pepper sports coat and a bolo tie with a silver horseshoe clasp. His black hair was shiny with tonic.

"Sport," he said to me. "I'd say you've been in some trouble."

"Trouble?" my mother said. "There's been no trouble here."

The Commodore pointed to my shirt pocket where a corner had been torn away in the melee at Kress's. "I don't imagine your mama sent you to school with your pocket like that. And that lip of yours. Looks a little fat to me. Like it got in the way of someone's fist."

"You might as well come clean," Dix said. She was wearing a lavender cowgirl dress with golden fringe along the bottom of the skirt. "You can't put anything past The Commodore."

A stray punch had clobbered me at Kress's, but I didn't want to admit any of this to The Commodore. Luckily, my mother came to my rescue. "Just a scuffle," she said. "You know boys."

"Tempers are on the boil," The Commodore said. "What with the nigras all up in the air. I hear there's been some nasty business downtown today."

My mother was always on edge whenever The Commodore was around, but on this afternoon, she looked close to coming apart. She bustled about, pulling out chairs for Dix and The Commodore at our dining table, going on and on about the eggshell we had just finished and what a funny thing it was that it was a miniature scene of people sitting around a dining table, and here we were sitting around a regular-sized table.

"Like a box inside a box," she said. "Or those hand-painted Russian dolls. Oh, you know the ones I mean. Take off the top half and there's a smaller doll inside. Five or six of them like that all the way down to the tiniest one — no bigger than the first joint of your pinky finger, Dix — and the funny thing is, even though the last one is so much smaller than the first one, their features are exactly the same."

The Commodore picked up "The Welcome Table" eggshell from its ornate stand, and held it with his thick fingers. "I bet there'd be something different," he said. "Something small, practically impossible to pick out. I bet I'd find it."

"Be careful with that," Dix said, and she said it with a hardness to her voice like a woman who had lived too long with a reckless man. "You bust that and Henny Penny might lose her head."

"It must take a world of patience." The Commodore set the eggshell back on its stand. "I'd say you'd have to have a ton of love to pay such close attention to things."

My mother ran her hand over our tablecloth. "Why, thank you, Commodore." A blush came into her face as if she were a young girl, unaccustomed to compliments. "That means a great deal, coming from someone with your keen eye."

It had been some time since my mother had been able to enjoy friends. In New Hampshire, when the truth of my father's mismanagement became public, she closed our blinds and refused to answer the telephone or the doorbell. Now, despite Dix's forwardness and The Commodore's suspicious nature, she was thankful for Nashville and the chance it had given her to be gracious and hospitable. When she came from our kitchen that afternoon, the serving tray held before her, the dessert cups filled with sherbet, the coffee cups chiming against their saucers, she might as well have been offering her soul to The Commodore and Dix, so desperate she was to have people admire her.

The Commodore had gone out on the porch to smoke a cigarette.

"Run, get The Commodore," my mother told me. "Tell him his sherbet's going to melt."

He was sitting on our porch glider, a cigarette hanging from his lip. He was reading a Glorious Days greeting card my father had left there. "Listen to this, Edward. 'May your special day be filled with sunshine and love.' Now that is a beautiful sentiment." He folded the card and tapped its spine against his leg. "Your daddy's not like me, is he?"

"No, sir. I suppose he's not."

"What you have to decide," he told me, "is whether that's a good thing."

I wanted my father to be noble and full of goodness. "He's been helping the Negroes organize the lunch counter demonstrations," I said.

The Commodore took a long drag on his cigarette. "How about you? What do you make of that?"

I touched my finger to my sore lip. "It's caused me some grief."

"Understand, I don't have anything against the nigras." He flipped his cigarette butt out into our yard. "But people here are set in their ways. I'm only telling you this for your own good. Whatever happens with this integration mess, your daddy has to live here."

When The Commodore said that, something lurched and gave inside me. The life we had invented for ourselves cracked and began to come apart. For the first time, I could see the raw truth of my family: we were cowards. If things didn't work out for us here, as they hadn't in New Hampshire, we could go somewhere else. We could choose a new name. We could do it as many times as we needed to — move away from ourselves, like opening one of those Russian dolls and finding another one inside. I saw us shrinking with each move we made until we got down to the smallest people we could be, the ones that wouldn't open, the ones made from solid wood.

The Commodore laid the greeting card on the porch glider. "Edward, your daddy ought to take care. You be sure to tell him what I said."

WE WERE eating sherbet when my father came home. We heard his car pull into the driveway, and my mother smiled and said to me, "How's that for luck? Your father's home early. Won't he be surprised to see we've got company?"

"Your husband?" Dix said. "My stars. We finally get to meet the mister."

My father came through the door and walked right up to the dining table and sat down across from The Commodore as if he had been expected. He kept his head bowed, and I could tell something was wrong. His hands were on the table, and his fingers were trembling, and the eggshell was wobbling on its stand. We all bowed our heads, as if we were asking a blessing, and for a long time, no one spoke.

Then my mother said, "Richard?" And she said it with the cautious tone I remembered from New Hampshire.

My father still wouldn't raise his head, and I'm not sure he even knew there were other people sitting at his table, people he didn't know, and wouldn't care for once he did. "I saw a boy killed today," he said, and his voice was barely a whisper. "That's all I want to say about it."

"Killed?" my mother said, and I think she knew, even then, that trouble had found us.

That's when The Commodore spoke. "An accident?"

Dix slapped his arm. "Mr. Thibodeaux said he doesn't want to say any more about it." When she said that, her voice steeled with warning, I could tell she had never gotten used to The Commodore's intimacy with accidents and deaths, hated him for it, no doubt, in ways she might not even have known.

But The Commodore wouldn't keep quiet. "I hope you weren't involved with it. That's all I'll say."

My father raised his face, and I could tell he was trying to hold himself together. His jaw was set, and his lips were tight, but his eyes were wet, and I could see he was crying.

"Probably some of that nigra mess," The Commodore said. "Is that it, pal?"

It was clear to me, then, that The Commodore hated something about my father, feared it, perhaps, and I decided it was the fact that my father was a careless man.

"If it is," The Commodore went on, "you asked for your trouble. Like those hotrodders who think the speed limit means everyone else but them. They don't see the danger. Buddy, you get out there on the wild side, something's bound to go wrong. Hell, you know it. I wouldn't think you'd have any call to cry over that."

"What's your name?" my father said to The Commodore. He turned to Dix. "Is this your husband?"

He wasn't crying now; his voice had that edge to it I recognized from the sit-in training sessions.

"His name's Commodore Gleason," Dix said. "We're friends of your wife. Dix and The Commodore."

"The Commodore's with the highway patrol," my mother said.

"He does accident reports," I told my father, hoping to explain The Commodore's interest in the boy's death, and somehow make my father feel better about all this.

"What do you do at an accident scene?" he asked The Commodore.

"I put it all together," The Commodore said. "Gather the facts, pal. Tell you how it happened."

"Talk to the survivors, do you?"

"That's right."

"Tell them you're sorry for their trouble?"

The Commodore gave a little laugh. "Say, what kind of a bastard do you think I am?"

"Do you mean it when you say it?" my father asked. "When you tell them you're sorry?"

"Listen, pal."

"Do you?"

"I'm there to get at the facts." The Commodore slapped his palm down on the table, and the eggshell wobbled again, and my mother put her hand to her mouth. "I'm there to get at the truth, pal. It's my job to know things." The Commodore stood up and pointed his finger at my father. "Just like I know what you're up to with the nigras. It's people like you who'll ruin the South. Even your own boy knows that. He's been clubbing niggers downtown today."

It's funny how your life slows down during the moments you wish you could speed away from and leave behind you forever. I could see the smallest details: the way the gold fringe on Dix Gleason's dress turned silver in the sunlight slanting through our window, my mother wetting her finger and rubbing at a spot of sherbet that had stained her white tablecloth, the way one string of The Commodore's bolo tie was shorter than the other, my father's shoulders sagging as if all the life had left him.

"Is that true, Ed?" he said to me.

I remembered the way I had shouted "nigger" at Kress's, how I had pushed my way out of the mob once the fighting had started. I had run outside, and had started walking, wanting to get as far away from Kress's as I could. I had walked and walked, and then I had caught a city bus and come home, and now The Commodore had lied about me, and because I felt so guilty about my part in the trouble downtown, because I wanted all this between The Commodore and my father to stop before it went too far, and The Commodore found out all there was to know about us — that our name wasn't Thibodeaux, that my father had made mistakes in New Hampshire, that we had tried our best to bury these facts — I said, yes, it was true.

My father slumped down in his chair. "I'm sorry," he said. "Folks, I'm sorry for all of this."

And The Commodore said, "Damn straight you're sorry. I could have told you that from the get-go."

THE BOY who died that day was not a Negro as we all had first believed. It was, as I would find out later, Dale Mink. He had come from Kress's, jubilant, the way he was after a basketball victory. He must have been feeling pretty full of himself. He was seventeen years old, a basketball star on his way to Vanderbilt, and he had the juice of a fist fight jazzing around in his head. When he ran out into the street, and saw my father's car, he must have been dazzled by how quickly misfortune had found him.

It was, my father finally told us, something he had played over in his head time and time again after he had told his story to the police: the street had been wet with rain, and the police vans had pulled up to Kress's. The officers were gathering up the black college students, arresting them for disorderly conduct, and the white boys who had attacked them were spilling out into the street. They were raising their arms and shaking their fists. My father glanced into his rearview mirror and noticed the way the skin was starting to wrinkle around his eyes. When he finally looked back to the street, there was Dale Mink, and it was too late for my father to stop.

My mother and I didn't know any of this when Dix and The Commodore left our house.

"He knows about you now," my mother said to my father. "He'll tell it over and over. And then where will we be?"

"Were you there?" my father asked me. "At Kress's?"

"I went with a boy from school. I didn't hit anyone. I said some things. That's all."

"You said things? Provoked those poor students? What did you say?"

I let my face go wooden, the way Lester Bates had when he had gripped the lunch counter, and the taunting had begun. "Things you taught me," I said.

My father lifted his hand, and with his finger, he brushed a piece of lint from his eyelashes. I wanted to think that he was an unlucky man — "Trouble knows my name," he had said in New Hampshire — but I could see he was actually a man of vanity. I knew that was a dangerous thing to be in the world. It meant forgetting others and concentrating only on yourself, and, when that was the case, all kinds of lunatic things could happen.

"I'm hungry," my father said. "I swear, Penny. I'm starved."

We were sitting at our dining table, and outside the light was fading. The eggshell was still upright in its stand, and what I remembered was how, when my father had first sat down, we had all bowed our heads and stared at it. I like to believe now that each of us, even The Commodore, was thinking, what a lovely scene. "Inviting," my mother had said earlier. The people around the miniature table seemed cozy and content. We must have looked at them with a desperate yearning. They were so small. They were so far away from us and everything that was about to happen in our home.

# SMALL FACTS

• • • • • • • •

GLEN HOBB brought his cream on Wednesday evenings when the Bethlehem Store was open until nine o'clock. He brought it in the back of his truck and wrestled the heavy cans into the store. He joked with Fern App, who tested the cream, then joined the other farmers who were loafing outside on the store's porch. If the old church pews were full, he squatted on his haunches, his back against a post. He lit one of the cigarettes he kept in a tin case, and waited.

From time to time, Fern glanced out the window to see if he was still there. Barn swallows scissored through the dusk. Calves bawled in the pastures. Corn pollen dusted the air, tassels just coming on.

Finally, the last light ebbed, and with a suddenness that always startled her, what had been bodies only moments before — boots and overalls and caps — vanished. And then there were only voices. She paid more attention then, listening for Glen's laugh, watching for the glow of his cigarette. She worried if she went too long without hearing him, or if she failed to see the ember at the end of his fingers, burning there in the dark.

At nine o'clock, when the other farmers had gone, he came into the store and helped her carry the cream cans to the storage locker. They rarely spoke, only an occasional nod or smile, or an "excuse me" from Fern — a blush — when staggering with the weight of a can, she bumped against him.

Then one Wednesday night, he said to her, "You're a touch older than I am, but I don't mind if you don't."

"I don't," she said.

And by Labor Day, they were married.


"HE HAS a farm," she told her sister Evie. "Glen Hobb. On the county line."

"It's all of a sudden," Evie said.

"Yes, you're right. But it's the thing to do."

"Will you still help me in the store?"

"Evie, I'm going to be a wife now."

"Well, of course. I see how it is. Just because I've never been married myself, doesn't mean I don't understand. You go on. I'll make out on my own."


THEY WERE married in the Olney Courthouse by the circuit judge. Glen wore a white shirt and freshly shined shoes. Fern worried that her slip might show or that her hose might run. Her new panty girdle squeezed her stomach and thighs until she felt faint. She was afraid to smile, lest she smudge her lipstick. She hoped she hadn't used too much powder or rouge, or dabbed too much cologne behind her ears.

Evie, who had come to stand as witness, squared her shoulders and planted herself, straight as a fence post beside her sister. Her eyes were hard set. She clutched her pocketbook to her ribs. The pocketbook was white, as was her dress and gloves and shoes.

"I suppose you must see something in him," she said to Fern after the ceremony.

"I do," said Fern.

She loved him because he had saved her from spinsterhood. Because he had given her a future. Because he was the first man to love her. For this favor, she felt she owed him.

BY EVENING, Glen had hauled all of Fern's belongings from the house she had shared all those years with Evie to his farm. Panties, brassieres, slips, cotton dresses, Zane Grey novels, a coffee can full of sand from Atlantic City, a Methodist hymnal, a Betty Crocker cookbook. "Well," he said. "Here we are. I've got chores to do. I eat my supper at six."

At six o'clock, he sat down to a meal of pan-fried ham, milk gravy, mashed potatoes, buttermilk biscuits, and for dessert, an apple pie.

Fern, anxious, nibbled at her food, glancing up from time to time to watch him eat. He weighed in, one elbow anchored on the table. He sawed off hunks of ham, sopped gravy with his biscuit.

When he finished, she brought him his pie and coffee. "My stars." He beamed at her. "My lucky stars. I must have married Betty Crocker herself."

She was full then. Full with love and good cheer. She breathed in the aromas of her cooking: cinnamon and nutmeg, butter and cream, the smoky cure of the ham, the clean wheat smell of flour.

Evie would be cooking soup beans. They would fill her kitchen with the dead smell of dried weeds. She would sit at her table, in the meager light, and peck at her supper.

But here there was substance. Here there was health and life. A man with an appetite, and a kind smile. Even his sneeze, a braying *gee-haw*, as if he were driving mules, gave her joy.

After supper, after she had washed and dried the dishes and tidied the oilcloth on the table, she joined Glen in the living room where he was watching *Matlock* on television. His shirt sleeves were rolled to his elbows; his legs were stretched out, his feet bare on the cool linoleum.

She sat next to him on the couch and memorized his scent. He smelled of the fields: of grain and wild onion, tilled earth and sweet clover. His hands, large and worn, had been fashioned for steering a tractor, prizing a pinch bar. Whorled skin shrivelled in the fleshy webs between his thumbs and forefingers. Calluses padded his palms, high up, at each finger's base, and purple veins inked the meaty hock of each thumb. She laid her hand in his palm, felt his strong fingers vise and clamp. She shuddered out of a joy and dread she did not understand until later when he took her to his bed and made love to her with a rough haste.

He was clumsy. He wrestled her the way he had the cream cans. He was accustomed to machinery and force. He had birthed calves, cut hogs. And while she was not prepared for his brawn, she did not resist it. She studied it, gave to it. She wrapped her arms around his back where springy hair mossed his shoulders and held to him. She felt a new world open to her. A world of men. Body and flesh. A world of passion and strength.

S H E   W O U L D not sew. She would cook and dust and launder. She would even help with chores. But under no circumstance would she touch a needle or thread.

Her hands were clumsy, her fingers like sticks. She could not sight thread through eye, and even if she managed, she did ugly patchwork: a series of botched stitches pulled too tight through the puckered cloth.

Rather than let Glen see this flaw she thought made her inadequate, she took her sewing to the store.

"Why should I sew for your man?" Evie asked the first time Fern came seeking her favor.

She sat behind the cash register, a fly swatter in her hand.

"Because you miss me." Fern was embarrassed by her honesty. "Because if you had the chance, you would have married Glen Hobb, too."

Evie laid the fly swatter on the counter. It was October, mid-afternoon. The farmers who had come in from the fields for bologna sandwiches, had gone. Their wives were either driving grain trucks or at home busy with chores. It was harvest time, the slow time at the store. Strips of flypaper twirled from the ceiling. The compressor of the meat cooler hummed. A wasp, one of the season's last, buzzed, trapped in the window, banging his head into the glass.

"Tell me about him," Evie said, and Fern understood a bargain had been sealed.

While Evie sewed on buttons and mended rips, Fern leaned across the counter and told her how Glen was quick with a joke, how before he smoked a cigarette he tapped each end on his watch crystal. She told her about the fine bones of his ankles. How he came in from the fields, dust and chaff stuck in the sweat on his neck. How he stood naked in the yard, while she poured water over his head.

She did not tell her about his rage, how his passion ran so deep, it brought up wellsprings of tears. Honest to goodness cried, he did. Sometimes because he could not loosen a nut, or find the proper tool. Because rain kept him out of the field, or equipment broke down. She did not tell her how she despised his tantrums, how she hated him when he came to her sobbing. He turned her from wife to mother and forced her, with his weakness, to be strong.

THE END of October came. Mornings, thin ice rimmed the puddles in the lane. The cattle — the shaggy roan bulls, the thoughtful jerseys — stayed close to the barn, hulking, their rubbery tongues working at salt licks.

Once, at dusk, a skein of geese passed over. Fern, toting fuel oil from the drum behind the hen house, stopped to watch. A dark vee arrowed across the low, clabbered clouds, honking, heading south. A sure sign that the killing frost was not far off. And then the winter with its short light, the frozen ponds, snow in drifts on the barren fields.

She boxed the last of the apples and squirreled them away in her pantry.

While the weather held, Glen hurried to bring in his corn. Fall rains had muddied the fields and kept him behind, and once he had been able to get into the bottom land he rented from Spec Tate, his picker had failed, an auger chain he had to replace.

One evening, a flock of geese came to feed on the corn stubble in the short field beyond the hog lot. Fern was coming from the hen house, eggs swaddled in her apron, when she heard the shotgun's crack. The raft of geese, squabbling, rose from the stubble. She swore she felt the air whirr with the urgent beating of wings.

Then Glen was loping in from the hog lot. His shotgun, broken and smelling of powder, was in one hand; a goose was in the other. He held it by its feet. Its long neck, lifeless, waggled and jounced. The black tips of its wings dragged the ground.

After supper, he brought her a pair of his cotton work gloves. The finger on one was torn, and needed mending.

She was on the wash porch, scalding the goose. Steam rose from the tub. The air was musty with the smell of wet feathers.

"I'll do it," she said.

He laid the gloves on her lap. "I need them tomorrow."

"I'm dressing your goose."

"I need them."

She let go of the goose and it dropped into the tub. Hot water splashed across Glen's legs. His hands balled into fists. He stepped toward her, just one step, but it was enough for her to feel his rage, to understand that he wanted to hit her. She could see it in the set of his jaw, the bunching of his brow. She felt a tender pity for him.

"You expect too much of me." She took his fists in her hands. The knuckles were scaly and cracked. "You all do. You men."

He was trying to understand. "You're my wife."

She remembered her mother. She knew the farm wives who came to the store. Their men counted on them. They expected them to make the phone calls, to keep the records. They asked them to do the milking, to feed the hogs and cows and sheep. Sturdy stock themselves, farm wives never got sick. They kept to their tasks, proud of their duty. Fern feared she had come to marriage too late to ever yoke herself to such service.

"Why did you marry me?" she asked.

Glen laughed, anger passing. "Because you said yes."

"No, really." This was important. She wouldn't let him off easy. "Why?"

She felt his fists pushing against her hands. She wondered if ever in his life, he had come this close to the truth, the kind of hard knowledge most people fence and guard.

He bowed his head. "I thought you might be my only chance."

Fear, then, had brought them together. Not loneliness, such as some had suspected. A mistrust of the future. A dread that they might come to one dark moment, where alone, they would regret their lives. Their union, Fern knew, had been insurance against that.

She nodded. "Me too."

Then she plucked the goose. Her fingers stripped the feathers down to the prickled flesh.

THE NEXT day, she was raking leaves when Evie came. She had piled them in the lane on the gravel, and Evie could drive her Ranger only as far as their ridge.

"You have to come with me," Evie said.

Fern tasted an oily smudge of coal at the corner of her mouth. Her coat and head scarf smelled of kerosene. "Look at me. I can't go anywhere. I look like I just crawled out of the woodpile."

The sun was weakening in the west, but the farmers were still in the fields. Their tractors — John Deeres and Olivers, Massey Fergusons and Internationals — filled the air with a throaty grumble, a growl that roiled the late afternoon calm.

Evie took the rake from Fern and tossed it into the weeds. "I told you." Her voice was stern. "Now. You have to come."

EVIE DROVE the county line road. She drove fast, and the rocks ridged in the middle spattered against the wheels and sprayed the fender wells. She gripped the steering wheel; Fern held her hands over her ears.

When they reached the blacktop, the Ranger's tires clicked over the seams the road crews had patched with tar. Only then, did Evie speak.

"Didn't you hear your phone?" she said. "They called and called."

"I was outside, down the lane."

"It's good for you they got me at the store."

Fern knew they were headed toward Olney. "It's Glen, isn't it?" she said.

Evie nodded. "It's Glen."

"The picker?"

"Yes."

They came up on the road crew. A skinny boy in an orange vest held out a red flag to stop them. Evie swung over on the shoulder and passed, dust flying.

"One hand or both?" Fern asked.

"No one knows the extent."

"*One* or *both*?"

Evie kept her eyes straight ahead. "You'll come out lucky in all this. Oh, don't look at me like I just said the most dreadful thing. It's only the truth. He needs you now. The rest of his life, he'll need you." She looked at Fern then, and her eyes were full of everything she felt for her sister, all her resentment and love. "That's what we want, isn't it? Sure it is. Someone who can't afford to let us go."

THE SURGEON wore canvas shoes and a sport shirt, a shirt with thin lapels that sliced a wide vee and laid bare his pink chest.

"We have taken the right hand here," he said and indicated the point of severance by laying a ballpoint pen across her wrist. "The left one . . ." He dropped the pen and had to squat to retrieve it. "We managed to save two fingers."

"Which two?" This was happening to her. This was her life changing, and she wanted all the facts.

The surgeon scratched his chest. "The thumb," he said, "and the index."

"Which is the index?" She turned to Evie. "I never remember."

Evie took her index finger and held it.

"He'll be out of the anesthesia soon," the surgeon said. "A while longer, and then you can see him."

"See him?"

"Of course, you'll want to see him."

"Yes," she said, and for the first time since Evie had come for her, she was afraid.

HE WAS groggy from the anesthesia, and sick. Fern held a bedpan for him, and he vomited green bile. His hair — she had never seen it so gray — was ruffled. A damp strand stuck to his forehead. His arms, stumps now, were swaddled in bandages and gauze. The two fingers the surgeon had saved poked out and spread themselves back and forth, working like pincers. She couldn't bear to watch them. They, much more than the stumps, reminded her of what had been lost. She closed her hand around them, and felt them go limp in her palm.

"An ear caught in the auger chain," he said. "And I tried to wrench it free."

The facts. Good, she thought. Facts were safe. She lifted the damp hair from his forehead and patted it onto his head.

"With your right hand?" She prompted.

"The auger chain took me in."

"And the left?"

"My hand was caught."

She could not squelch a note of resentment. One hand could have been saved. "You should have kept the left one out." She let go of his fingers and turned to the window. The sun was going down. It would be a clear night, cold, with a hard frost.

"It was my hand. I had to try to save it."

"It was gone," she said.

"The glove," he told her. "The tear. That's what the auger caught."

GANGRENE set in. Fever, and a putrefaction of tissue in his stumps. The room smelled of it. Fern sat by his bed and breathed the stench of his rotting flesh.

"They're going to take more, aren't they?" he asked.

"Tomorrow morning." She knew she owed him the truth. "Three inches above the right wrist, two above the left."

He closed his eyes a moment. A gurney clacked by outside in the hallway. He swallowed and said, "I'm thirsty."

She held the straw to his lips so he could drink. In that one gesture, she saw the future laid out before them. Two days before, she had been a woman raking leaves, planning supper for her husband: pork chops and butternut squash, a coconut cream pie for dessert. Then Evie had come in her Ranger.

A tear in a glove.

A remnant of cloth.

The small facts of disaster.

As Glen sucked at the straw, she felt herself give to the binding power of loss. He would sleep that night in fits. At intervals, he would wake and call her name, not alarmed, but inquiring, asking her to announce her presence. She would answer with a hand pressed to his shoulder. And in that way, she would tell him she was there, and would be in the morning when the orderlies came.

# THE END OF SORRY

●     ●     ●     ●     ●     ●     ●     ●

A FEW DAYS before Christmas, in 1959, my father shot a man named Lyle King, and would have killed him, if not for a quirk of anatomy which had located Mr. King's heart an inch to the left of where by rule it should have been. "Joe," my father told me some time later, "I meant to kill that sonofabitch, and I would have — no joke — if only his heart had been in the right place."

My mother was in love with Lyle King, though at the time my father shot him, I didn't know that. I thought my father shot him because they had different notions about how a man was best to live his life. My father, Lyle King said, was a scab. "You're holding back the working man," he said. "You must be a communist." "No, I'm no communist," my father said. "I'm just trying to look out for my wife and my son."

Nineteen fifty-nine, in southern Indiana, was not a good time for farmers. A summer drought had brought on a lean winter, and when the packing house workers in town went out on strike, and my father had a chance to hire on as a replacement, he did.

"We're in hog heaven now," he said. "Happy days."

Years later, my mother would tell me we would have been all right that winter — the drought hadn't left us as short as my father liked to let on. "He was restless," she would say. "We were both restless. I guess we wanted a little jazz."

My father was a sticker on the killing floor. It was his job to slice open two arteries in a hog's throat. It took a sure, quick hand, he told me, to make the cuts and ensure a clean bleed. "You see that blade," he said to me one night as he was showing me the long knife he kept in a scabbard on his belt. "Can't even tell it's been used, can you? Not a speck of blood on it. A good sticker pulls out a clean knife, Joe. Remember that."

It would be awhile before I would be afraid for him. Even though he hinted at the danger he had put himself in, I couldn't imagine it. It seemed like something out of the movies, the drama of someone else's life.

"Men are angry," he said just before Christmas. "Men I've known for years. You wouldn't want to hear the ugly things they shout at me. Sometimes I think they'd like to kill your old man. Honest, I do. Good men, Joe, who used to have better sense."

At first I didn't think of him as a scab. I was seventeen, and I guess I didn't think of him in any way at all. He was Glen Piper, and for the most part, I didn't think his life and the choices he made in it had anything to do with me.

My best friend that year was a boy named Ray Marsh. His father had given him a rig of steel traps, and we had laid out a drowning set along the creek west of town. Each trap was chained to a wire, stretched taut from a stake on the creek bank to a sandbag anchored along the bed. Once caught, muskrats and beavers would dive and follow the wire into the water. When they realized they were in too deep, they would try to swim back to the surface, but their own motion would trip a stop-slide L-bracket. It would crimp against the wire and hold them underwater where they would drown.

It took some smarts and know-how to rig a drowning set — to choose the proper gauge and length of wire — and that suited Ray since he had always had a head for science and mathematics. He was a slender boy with sunken cheeks, and unlike me, he was a good student who was always figuring problems, his fingers busy with a pencil. I envied his tidy numbers written on a sheet of notebook paper and his sweet, peaceful look when he would finally come to an answer. When I was with him, I somehow sensed I was as whole as I would ever be, and I don't mind saying I loved Ray Marsh and his faith that any problem could be solved and put to rest.

Each morning before school, we slipped into the woods and checked our drowning set. I carried a .22 caliber handgun in case we ever came upon a problem catch — a fox or coyote caught in a leghold trap, waiting for us on the bank — but I had never used it. We pulled the traps to the surface and emptied them and sold our pelts to the fur trader in town. We passed by the packing house those gray winter mornings and saw the strikers gathered around fires burning in fuel oil drums.

Ray's father was a union steward, and one morning he stepped out on his porch and said to me, "Joe, I think it would be better if you didn't come back to my house." Denton Marsh was a tall man who wore string ties and cowboy shirts with pearl buttons. "It's an ugly time. Men want to know who they can trust. You understand."

Later at school, Ray said he had brought in a mink that morning. "I'll save your half of the pelt money," he told me. He was saving his to buy a sheepskin coat. "Don't worry, Joe. Our dads have got us in a pinch for a while, but this strike won't last forever. Pretty soon, we'll know what we've got here, and then everything will be all right."

MY FATHER started carrying my .22 for protection. It was still loaded with the solid point shorts I had anticipated needing for close range shots, bullets that wouldn't expand on contact like hollow points and damage a pelt. "It's a sad state of affairs," my father said, "when a man has to come to this. I always meant to live a peaceful life."

After he had died, my mother would say she never believed him when he said that, not for a minute. "He could be a cruel man, your father. You probably don't remember him that way."

I remember him as a good man who could have lived a decent life if circumstances had been other than what they were. I suppose he took things to heart more than most men, and maybe that's what eventually cost him, cost all of us, I guess, in ways I still can't fully explain. He had a sweet, baritone voice, and for a while he had sung with a gospel quartet and had even made an album once in a recording studio in Nashville. Some Sundays in church, when his voice was particularly fine, he would hit the chorus of "When the Roll Is Called up Yonder," and honest-to-goodness tears would come to his eyes. Before the strike, he called square dances at the community center on Saturday nights, and he told me once he could look out at Texas stars, the dancers turning to his call, and for a moment, he could be stunned — "pole-axed" — by the sheer beauty of it all. "This can be a grand life, Joe," he told me once. "If we'll let it."

"He was always talking sweet like that," my mother would say later. "Why do you think I fell for him? But really, Joe, he never believed the half of it."

The truth is my father was a man of regrets. He was sorry, he used to say, he hadn't gone with his brother to work in the steel mills of East Chicago instead of staying behind to tend his daddy's farm. "A farm can eat you alive, Joe. It can turn you sour and fill you up with mean spirits." And he was sorry he hadn't gone to the service and seen some of the world during the war instead of opting for a farmer's deferment: "Other men have stories, Joe. They've had different lives. Sometimes I hate those men. I know it's a lousy thing to say, but I can't help it. Your old man can be a cussed, spiteful mule."

That winter, he had reached the end of sorry and had given himself over to the other side of regret — a pure, sharp rage — and when I watched him handle his knife or speak ill of the packing house workers on the picket line, I suspected he had made friends with his anger and didn't care what happened, wanted things to happen, even — ugly things he barely dared imagine.

"It feels like everything's set to go sky-high," he said one night as he was cleaning the .22. "That's why I keep this handy. In case someday I need it."

IT WAS about this time that my mother went to work for the Assessor's Office at the county courthouse. She had held a job before in her life and it was something she enjoyed. Before she met my father, she worked as a telephone operator at the switchboard in town. "Oh, she was an operator all right," Lyle King would say after he had recovered from his gunshot wound. "She moved right in and set up shop."

When she worked at the telephone company, she owned a second-hand Ford and had it washed every Friday afternoon at the Texaco station where she enjoyed the attendants' shy glances and the way they would stumble over one another to light her cigarettes. She wore linen suits and open-toed pumps and nylon stockings purchased at the Janet Shop downtown. She had a closet full of blouses and jackets and lingerie items that came in slim boxes with tissue paper wrapping folded over inside. Her dressing table was scattered with lipstick in slim, gold tubes, and tins of rouge, and atomizers filled with Lily of the Valley cologne. Each morning she sat in her slip and robe and painted her face. She drew a beauty mark just above her lip with an eyebrow pencil. She sprayed a mist of cologne into the air and walked through it.

Of course, I don't know whether any of this is true, but even now I imagine it is because in 1959 my mother, at the age of forty, was still slim and attractive and knew how to make a man notice her.

"I wasn't looking for trouble," Lyle King told me once. "But, brother, I wasn't dead either."

LYLE KING was the County Assessor. It was his job, he always said, to know shitholes from applesauce. He appraised properties and assigned values and levied taxation. My mother went to work in his office preparing tax statements. "He keeps me hopping," she told me one night. "Some people think he's a gouger, but I think he's a good man — a Democrat. His father went belly up during the Depression. 'A penny matters,' he always says, 'especially when you have to work for it.' "

I had never thought much about Lyle King before then. My father said he was a man who had gone away and made good only to come back and rub people's noses in it. When my father wasn't around, my mother would talk about Lyle King and tell me things I imagined he had shared with her in confidence. As a young man, he had won a scholarship to the Oakland City Teacher's College and had come back to teach bookkeeping and typing and shorthand at the high school before opening his own accounting office and then running for County Assessor. For a while, during the war, he had gone to Chaplain's Training School at Fort Benjamin Harrison, until an Army doctor had found out about his heart. "It's out of kilter," my mother said. "Ripley's 'Believe It or Not!' even wrote a piece up on him. You know, an odd fact. He carries the newspaper clipping in his billfold. Maybe someday, Joe, he'll let you see it."

My father and Lyle King were different sorts of men, and what I was learning that winter was that there were men other men ridiculed, thought useless and light in the balls. To my father, Lyle

King was one of those, and the fact that my mother had gone to work for him, spoke highly of him, no less, caused something blood-red and hurtful to boil up between them.

"Lyle King," my father said one night. "He's about as worthless as tits on a boar."

ONE NIGHT Lyle King came to our house for supper. My father had started working overtime by then, and most nights it would be dark, far past six, when I would see his headlights coming up our lane.

Lyle King arrived at five-thirty. He knocked on our front door, a polite tapping, and my mother took off her apron, and patted her hairdo, and ran her tongue over her lips to moisten them. She was wearing a pair of orange slacks — capri pants, she called them — and a white blouse with a ruffled front. I couldn't imagine anyone being disappointed to have her waiting there in the middle of our living room, anxious to greet them. "Go on, Joe," she said. "Open the door."

When I opened the door, Lyle King was polishing his glasses with his handkerchief. He stepped into our house, squinting and blinking, and when he had finally settled his glasses back on his face, he eyed my mother and said, "Well, hello, Rosalie. You look like Fort Knox."

His trouser legs were stuffed into his galoshes. He was wearing a wool overcoat and a long, green scarf coiled around his throat.

"Lyle, you look like you're ready for rough weather," my mother said. "My word, let's get you unwrapped. I want you to feel at home."

Lyle King had never married. The rumor was he had been engaged once, but the girl had run off with a travelling photographer, and after that, Mr. King had begun to develop a lust for finery and swank. Each year, he ordered a new car from the Oldsmobile dealer, always a 98, emerald green, with rolled leather seats. He wore double-breasted suits, custom-tailored in St. Louis, and he owned a beach house in Florida where he went on vacation a few weeks every winter.

I suppose my mother and I were among the few who suspected Lyle King's extravagant tastes were smokescreens. We had seen him once pull his 98 into his driveway, and before he shut off the engine, he bent forward, bowed his head, and let it rest on the steering wheel. The front of his fedora lifted up, and the hat slid a ways down his neck. He looked as if he had hit something head-on, and the impact had pitched him forward, and now he was stunned and helpless, slumped over the steering wheel. Or maybe, one might have concluded, he had been very tired and had stopped to rest. It was easy to imagine that he would wake soon, and look around him like a man who had been lost for a while and was just then trying to figure out where he was and what he had been doing the moment before he had fallen asleep. "He must think his life is a lonely life," my mother had said, and though I thought nothing of it at the time, I imagine that must have been the moment she began to fall in love with him.

"You look like a mummy," she said to him that night in our living room. She stepped up close to him and unwrapped the green scarf from around his throat. "There." She smoothed the lapels of his overcoat. "At least now you can breathe."

Lyle King took a deep breath and let it out. "Something smells delicious, Rosalie."

"We're having chicken," my mother said. "Just an old yard hen, but I've rolled it in Ritz cracker crumbs and spiced it up with paprika and parmesan cheese. I call it, 'Chicken Puttin' on the Ritz.' "

"Your mother's a gem." Lyle King winked at me. "She can make the hum-drum seem out of this world."

When he said that, I could see he admired something bright and exciting about my mother, something he knew from his work with her at the Assessor's Office, and though I was in my own house, I felt like strange company, come uninvited into other people's lives.

"Help Mr. King with his coat and galoshes, Joe," my mother said, "while I finish up our supper."

Lyle King slipped off his galoshes and left them on the mat by the door. He laid his overcoat across the back of my father's easy chair. "You're Joe." He firmed up the knot in his necktie and glanced around our living room. I imagined him taking in the rose-print wallpaper, the green linoleum, the couch with its fringed chenille throw cover, and for the first time in my life, I was ashamed of my home. "You and that Marsh boy are trappers."

"We were," I said.

"Were?"

"That's right."

"Say no more." Lyle King held up his hand. "I got it. Your father's stirred things up for you, made it rough with your friends."

He sat down on our couch and smiled at me as if he knew everything there was to know about my life. "A man ought to be ready to live with what he shows the world of himself." He draped his arms along the back of the couch, and his suit jacket gaped open, and his necktie puffed up in the middle as if it had suddenly filled with air. "That's what I'd like to tell your father. Maybe I could save him some grief."

I thought of my father driving home in the dark, the .22 on the seat beside him. I heard my mother in the kitchen humming "Anything Goes," and Lyle King smiled again. He leaned over and picked up a knickknack from the coffee table — a ceramic trinket my uncle had sent us from Biloxi, Mississippi. It was half of a chamber pot, and on the front, in blue letters, it said, "For All My Half-Assed Friends." Lyle King held the chamber pot at arm's length and tipped back his head so he could read it through his bifocals.

"I've done some travelling myself," he said. "I've seen a good deal of this country. In fact, I've seen some odd things. Things most people wouldn't believe. I went to California once and saw a place called 'The Mystery Spot.' It's up in the Santa Cruz Mountains among the redwood trees. Some of those trees are over three hundred feet tall, by the way. I've seen trees so big around the road makers had to hollow out the trunks and lay the roads right through them. I'm not kidding you, brother. I've driven a car through a tree." He looked at the chamber pot again and chuckled. Then he set it back on the coffee table. "But what I want to tell you about is this place. This 'Mystery Spot.' Animals won't come near it. The trees there grow like corkscrews. A ball will roll uphill — *up*hill, Joe — and a compass needle will spin in circles. I tried my best to stand up straight when I was there, and it was impossible. I kept tipping forward. When I tried to walk, I reeled like a Saturday night drunk. Some people say there's a piece of star buried there and it gives off magnetic signals. I don't know about that. But it was a screwy place. The laws of nature went right out the window. I've never felt so helpless." He shook his head as if he were still trying to figure it out. "What can you trust, Joe?" He thumped his chest. "My own heart. Even it's not where it's supposed to be."

"My mother says you were in Ripley's 'Believe It or Not!' "

"The world can be a strange place, Joe. Take this strike for instance. It's trouble. A real powder keg. Who knows what might happen? I don't know about you, but, brother, I'm ready for anything."

WHEN MY FATHER came home, he brought in the cold air and the gamy smell of the packing house: a blend of scalded hog bristles, and steaming entrails, and a rusty smell I imagined to be the scent of blood. He was wearing a corduroy coat, the collar turned up around his ears, and he had his arms wrapped around his chest, and he was shivering.

"Jesus, it's cold," he said. "I can't get warm."

"It's cozy here," said Lyle King. "I was just chatting with your son."

My father took a step toward his easy chair and saw Lyle King's overcoat. "You've come for supper," he said, as if he were just then recalling why Lyle King was in our house.

"That's the ticket." Lyle King snapped his fingers together. "We're having chicken. Something special your wife dreamed up. What is it, Joe?"

"Chicken Puttin' on the Ritz," I said.

My father picked up Lyle King's overcoat and carried it to him. "Put this on," he said. "I want you to come outside. I want to show you something. You, too, Joe. Get your coat. I tell you, it's cold out there."

Outside, I followed my father and Lyle King through our gate to where my father's truck and Lyle King's Oldsmobile were parked beneath a pole light. The night was frigid and still, and already frost had started to form in cracks and webs on the Oldsmobile's windshield. I could hear every sound, sharp and clear: the buckles jangling on Lyle King's galoshes, my father's scabbard slapping against his leg, the hum of the pole light. We walked into its glow, and my father pointed to a spot on the door of his truck just below the handle. "Look at this," he said to Lyle King. "Go on. Give me your best guess at what it means."

Lyle King bent at the waist and pushed his glasses up on his nose. "That scratch?" He straightened and put his hands in his pockets. "I'd say you got too close to something, Glen."

My father laughed. "That shows what you know, Mr. County Assessor. I'd say a knife point did that." He took his own knife from its scabbard and scraped the point over the truck's door. He gouged it into the paint until the primer coat showed in the gash. "Joe, that's the work of those union goons. That's their way of telling me to watch out."

"If you think that's what that is," Lyle King said, "it's no wonder. How do you expect those men to treat you? I was just telling Joe . . ."

"Joe doesn't need to hear your union claptrap." My father pointed his knife at Lyle King. "He'll find out what it takes to get ahead. He'll look out for himself. He won't need some gang of thugs to do it for him."

When he said that, I felt ashamed of the things I had started to believe about him, that he was cold-blooded and devil-may-care. I imagined, more than anything, he was lonesome, and I decided I would stick by him and be his friend.

"You've never had to sweat much for a dollar," my father said to Lyle King. "But now you think you know what's best for the ones of us who do."

"All I'm saying, Glen, is that a man deserves a decent wage, especially for a job like that."

"Like that?" my father said. "What do you know about it? Have you ever been in that packing house? Here, let me show you how I stick a hog." He stepped up to Lyle King, then, and put the tip of his knife to his throat right above the green scarf. "If I was to kill a man, I'd get him right here. Just like a hog. Bleed him clean."

Lyle King's shoulders went back. "Why in the world would you want to kill a man, Glen?"

"I'm not saying I'd want to, only that I could if it came to that."

"I feel sorry for someone who would think that way."

My father took his knife away from Lyle King's throat. "I don't want you to feel sorry for me."

"Well, I do. It's the truth of things."

I got the picture, then, of Ray Marsh setting aside pelt money for me, and it gave me a sick feeling to think of him looking at me as a charity case.

My mother stepped out on our porch and called to us. "Boys, it's getting lonely in here," she said, and my father put his knife back in his scabbard, and then the three of us went in where it was warm to eat our supper.

A FEW DAYS later, I ditched my afternoon classes and went to the creek and used a pair of snips to cut the wires on the drowning set. I sprung the steel traps and threw them into the water, and when I was done, I sat down on a fallen log along the creek bank, and I got shaking cold all over because I knew my life was going to change, had caught me already in a snare I hadn't seen coming and probably couldn't have avoided even if I had.

The next morning at school, Ray said to me, "Someone's ruined our set. Cut the wires and taken the traps. Whoever it was must not think much of themselves. To do something like that. They must want their lives to be ugly. It makes me feel sad for them." He handed me an envelope. "I'm sorry, Joe. It looks like we're out of business. Here's your half of the pelt money."

"You keep it," I said. "I wasn't much of a trapper."

"No, it's yours." He slipped the envelope into my shirt pocket. "You were a good scout. You earned it."

The rest of the day, I felt low-down and no-good, and though I knew if I would only confess to Ray he would forgive me, I couldn't bring myself to do it. The night my father had put his knife to Lyle King's throat, something had emptied inside me, some faith I had managed that in the ragged hours of regret the world would find a way to remind us that goodwill and love had been, and would still be, our regular come and go. Ray Marsh had surrounded me with that faith, and my father had sliced through it and bled it dry.

"A man has to keep his pride, Joe," he had said to me that night when Lyle King had gone. "That's all he's got, really, when you get down to it. I suppose I'd do almost anything to save it."

IT WAS our custom in those days to go to town on Saturday nights. We would eat supper at the cafe, and then my mother would get her hair done at Ellis Green's Looking-Glass, and I would hook up with Ray Marsh, and my father would make his way over to the community center to call the square dance.

But, of course, once he had gone to work at the packing house, that had all changed. "They don't want your old man calling their dances anymore," he said. "They think I'm poison. Some goddamn leper."

Denton Marsh was the new caller. "He's as dry as last summer," my father said. "Dancing for him is like doing arithmetic. Left foot here, right foot there. Might as well be a la-de-dah cakewalk."

The last Saturday before Christmas, we came out of the cafe and saw a tire gone flat on my father's truck.

"I'd like Lyle King to see that," he said. "Wouldn't you, Joe? I'd like to know what he thinks of his union boys now."

A sharp wind was shooting straight down Main Street, and

pine flockings and tinsel Christmas stars were dancing and rustling on the streetlight poles. My mother settled a scarf on her
head and tied it beneath her chin. The scarf was turquoise blue
with aqua peacocks printed on it. "That's just a flat," she said.
"From the looks of things, you probably picked up a nail."

"Sure." My father cupped his hands and blew into them.
"That's what that is. That's just a nail. Or maybe someone helped
that tire go flat. Bled it through the valve stem."

My mother stamped her foot. "You," she said. She was wearing
a new pair of snow boots with rabbit fur around the tops. "You
want us to feel sorry for you, don't you? Poor Mr. Woe-Is-Me."

"I'm just looking at the facts, Rose." My father got the jack out
from the well behind the truck seat. "I could use a hand here,
boss," he said to me. "Rose, go on back to the cafe. I'll put on the
spare, and then I'll take you to Ellis Green's. Joe and I can get the
flat patched at the station, and then come and get you. Isn't that
the way we should do it, Joe?"

My mother glanced back at the cafe. At tables and booths,
people had turned to watch us. Through the steam-covered
windows, they looked watery and small and far away. "I won't go
back in there," my mother said. "You must hate me. You must
hate both of us, Joe and me. You must want our lives to be
difficult."

"Your mother thinks I hate you," my father said to me. He was
crouched down at the back of the truck. He was wedging the jack
in under the axle. "Have you ever thought that, Joe? That I'd do
anything but love you? My God. What a thing to say."

"I'm not going back in there," my mother said again. "I'll walk to the Looking-Glass. You can pick me up when I'm done. That is, if you care to."

My father straightened from his crouch. "Why sure, Rose. I'll come for you." He put his hands on his hips and looked at me. "What about you, Joe? What are you going to do?"

I couldn't stand the thought of being at the service station when my father brought in the flat tire. I knew how the attendants would smirk, how they would rib him — "Glen, it looks like you've been *stuck*."

"It's a lonely walk in the cold," I said. "I guess I'll go with Mom."

"Now I know what you think of me," my father said. "That's good. I wouldn't want to have the wrong idea of myself. Now it's out in the open. Now we know exactly where we stand."

ELLIS GREEN was a retired barber who had opened up the Looking-Glass Hair Shop in the front of his home. He cut both women's and men's hair, but my father always said the only sort of man who would go there would have to be a fellow with no lead in his pencil. What kind of man, he wanted to know, would sit in the same room with a bunch of squawking hens and let old Ellis Green take scissors to his hair when Tubby Simms, uptown, would provide a complimentary King Edward cigar and the latest copy of *The Police Gazette* to his regular customers.

I had always liked Ellis Green. He had a white moustache, immaculately groomed, and the top of his head, where the hair was thin, was freckled with age spots. He wore sleeve garters to keep his cuffs off his wrists and a green eyeshade, the kind I had seen card players wear in movies. I had no reason to share my father's contempt of him and his shop. In fact, when it was summer, and the Cardinals were playing baseball, I liked to sit on the front porch in the glider and listen to Harry Caray's radio broadcasts coming out through Ellis Green's screen door.

On this night, when my mother and I stepped into the shop, Rosemary Clooney was singing "Come On-a My House" on the radio, and Lyle King was sitting in the barber chair, his face white with shaving cream.

"Rosalie," he said. "You look like an orphan in a storm."

"Mercy sakes, Miss Piper," said Ellis Green. He was honing a razor on the leather strop attached to the side of the chair. "Have you lost your sense? It's wicked cold out there. Too cold to be out in it for long. What's the matter with that Glen Piper, he don't take care of you better than this?"

My mother took off her scarf and walked up to Lyle King and put her hands on his face. She laid her hands on the hot shaving cream, and wisps of steam lifted from Lyle King's cheeks. "Are my hands cold?" she wanted to know.

Lyle King just looked at her, as if for once he didn't know what to make of something.

"Miss Piper, you've ruined a good lather," said Ellis Green. "Now what's poor Mr. King to do?"

AFTER LYLE KING's shave, he sat down beside me and rubbed his hand over his face. "A close shave makes a man feel like a million bucks, Joe. Like his stock's gone up and everyone's a buyer. I believe I'll sit here awhile and enjoy it before I go back out in the cold."

He smelled of Wildroot hair tonic and talcum powder. He was wearing a red sweater, buttoned just over his stomach, and his white shirt showed in the wide vee the sweater cut over his chest.

For some reason, I wanted to tell him what I had done to Ray Marsh's drowning set — Lyle King was that sort of man, someone who understood the way people could sometimes fall short of their own worth — but then he said, "Joe, your mother is a lovely woman. I think Ellis is right. Your father ought to look out." My mother's scarf was on the chair beside Lyle King, and he picked it up and folded it into a neat square, something I couldn't imagine my father doing. "When you've got something of value, you've got to keep an eye on it. I know that. I lost someone dear to me once. The one thing I know is people are greedy. I suppose you know that, too. I guess these days it's a fact."

My mother didn't hear any of this because by this time she was sitting in a chair with her head tipped back over Ellis Green's sink. He was washing her hair, wetting it with the spray nozzle, and when she finally raised her head, and saw Lyle King, she said, "Are you still here? Goodness, I don't want you to see me like this."

Of course, when she said that, giggling the way girls did at school when they talked about the boys they liked, I should have known she was in love with Lyle King, had taken her life to a point where all sorts of unexpected things could happen, but I wouldn't register that fact until later. Then, I just thought she was embarrassed to have Lyle King see her with her hair wet, squashed down, and sticking to her head in ringlets and curls.

"Why sure I'm still here," Lyle King said. "I'm waiting to see if Glen remembers you. I want to make sure you're taken care of, Rosalie. You and Joe."

LATER, I would think that only if my father had come for us when he had said he would, our lives, from then on, would have been familiar and less burdensome. But maybe, like my mother said later, that night wasn't the start of our misery, but only our troubles catching up to us.

"I've been stood up," she said when my father didn't show. "Maybe I'm a single woman now. Is that what you think, Lyle?"

"I don't know what to think," he said. "But I know I've got my 98 right outside, and I'm going to go out there now and warm it up, and then I'm going to take you and Joe uptown. Is that all right with you, Rosalie?"

My mother looked at me and shrugged her shoulders. "What can I do, Joe? He's my boss."

The 98 was warm when we got into it, and I could smell the leather seats and the rich smell of Lyle King, a scent of wool, and freshly laundered shirts, and Old Spice aftershave. The front seat was roomy, and my mother slid over next to Lyle King. "Don't sit in back, Joe." She patted the seat. "Sit up front with the family."

There was a compass on Lyle King's dashboard. "That's so I'll know where I'm going," he said. "I wouldn't want to get lost, would you, Rosalie?"

It was close to ten o'clock when Lyle King turned down Main Street and drove past the community center. My father's truck was there, parked beneath a streetlight. A group of men had gathered around it, and in their midst I could see my father and Denton Marsh. My father was poking Denton Marsh in the chest with his finger, and Denton Marsh was letting him do it. He was standing there in his shirtsleeves, a cowboy hat pushed back on his head.

"This doesn't look good," Lyle King said, and then he pulled the 98 to the curb.

When the three of us got over to where my father and Denton Marsh were standing, I heard my father say, "You know something about this, and I expect you to make it right."

Denton Marsh held up his hands and chuckled. "Whoa, hoss," he said to my father. "I told you. I wouldn't know anything about someone taking a knife to your tire. You're the sticker."

I thought maybe he meant his remark in good humor, a joke to take some of the heat out of the moment, but of course, my father didn't hear it that way. His head was bare, and his ears were red, and he bumped Denton Marsh with his chest. "Do you think I'm a fool?" he said.

The other men moved back a few steps, and my father and Denton Marsh were by themselves for a while. Then Lyle King stepped up to my father, and he said, "I do. That's exactly what I think you are, carrying on like this and your wife and son here to see it."

My father looked around then, and saw my mother and me standing on the sidewalk.

"Rose," he said.

My mother hadn't bothered with her scarf in Lyle King's 98, and with her fresh hairdo and her gold snap-on earrings, she looked as if she had been called away from something festive and gay.

"I waited, Glen," she said. "You must be surprised to see me here."

My father raised his arm and pointed at me. "There's my boy," he said. "He'll tell you the truth about this."

"There's no need to drag Joe into this," Lyle King said. "There's only one thing to do. Let's have a look at that tire and see what's what."

My father hoisted the tire out of the truck bed and set it on the ground. "Look here," he said. Then he looked right at me. "A nail didn't do this."

Lyle King squatted down and fingered a flap of rubber where a knife had plunged in and caught the inner tube and ripped a gash, and I knew in an instant that sometime after my mother and I had left my father he had done that, and it made me sorry for him because somehow he had lost whatever had once been right-thinking and optimistic about the way he saw his life. He had cut free from it, had given up the true, good part of himself he had more than likely sworn he would know forever.

"It's been cut all right," said Lyle King. "Anyone can see that. The only question is who's to blame."

It was then that I spotted Ray Marsh at the edge of the crowd. He was wearing the sheepskin coat he had saved his pelt money for, but it was too big for him. The hem came down to his knees, and his fingers barely showed at the ends of his sleeves. Something about that coat and the way he stood there, hangdog, waiting to see what his father would do, made me sick with shame, and because I loved my father and wanted us to be the sort of men who would always own up to the wrong we had done, I said, "My father's right. I know something about this."

At that moment, the mystery of who had destroyed the drowning set must have cleared for Ray. He stepped forward, and he pointed his finger at me. "It was you," he said.

I felt the sweet relief of confession wash over me. "That's right," I said. "I'm the one who did it."

The men in the crowd started to laugh, and I understood they thought I was confessing to slashing the tire. They were laughing at my father, at a man whose own son could betray him, and he let go of the tire and it fell over and wobbled at his feet.

Lyle King stepped up on the truck's running board and raised his arms and waved them about until the crowd went still: "At least Joe's got enough decency to admit it when he's done something he shouldn't have. That's more than I can say for you, Glen. I'm surprised you'd have the nerve to come here and accuse these men. You're taking food from their tables the way it is, and you don't give a tinker's dam. Even your wife knows that. She's told me as much."

"I don't want to hear you talk about my wife," my father said.

"I'm going to tell you something." Lyle King stepped down from the running board. "And you're going to listen. Glen, I'm going to tell you exactly the way things are."

And that's when my father pulled the .22 from his coat pocket and shot Lyle King in the chest.

YEARS AND YEARS have gone by since then, but still I can remember the most unusual things. I remember that one of my mother's gold earrings mysteriously fell to the street, and my father staggered forward a few steps before he stooped and laid the .22 on the slashed tire. I remember Lyle King stumbled backward, away from my father, and sat down on the truck's running board. "You've shot me, Glen," he said, as if he were amazed by it all. "It hurts to be shot. I can tell you that. It hurts like hell."

Even now, when all along I have known this point in my story would come, it stuns me. "People can do crazy things," my mother would say much later after Lyle King had survived, after my father had gone to Vandalia State Prison, and my mother had divorced him and moved us to Evansville where she would marry a man I would never know since by that time I would be living away from her in California. Until she died, I would call her each year at Christmas, and she would make me promise to do a better job of keeping in touch. "We can lose ourselves," she would say. "We can slip away, just like that, before anyone can figure out how to save us."

But that night, when my father shot Lyle King, all she could do was put her arms around me and hold me to her. "This isn't your fault, Joe." Though I loved my mother and father, felt a renewed tenderness for them, even, already they had started to seem strange to me, as if they were people I had known a long time ago and would never know again. "Someday you'll have to make up your mind about your father and me."

I could see Denton Marsh crouched over Lyle King, and my father standing in the street. He held his arms out straight before him. "My God," he said in a loud voice. "Look at me. My hands are shaking."

When he said that, I knew that he was scared, wanted to get back to safe ground, as I did, his only son, terrified by what had just become the beginning of my life.

I can still see us in the cold night, can hear the sheriff's siren in the distance. Both of us lifted our heads like animals startled by twigs snapping, frozen in that moment when they sense they're not alone, magnificent and still in that instant of pause — splendid and untouchable — before nerves twitch, and they run.

# SECRETS

• • • • • • • •

ACH HALF HOUR, Oren goes outside and shines his flashlight on the thermometer tacked to the front of the house. He leaves the door open, and Glenna, dishes done, smells rain, hopes it will be gentle when it comes — a steady, soaking rain to last the night.

She knows he is not checking the temperature, that the thermometer is only an excuse, that what he is really doing is listening for the dogs: Moad Keen's hounds, no respecters of crops and gardens, set loose three nights this week, chasing fox.

"If they come through here tonight," Oren has promised, "I'll be ready." His rifle, a Remington .30-.30, is leaning against his recliner. His crossword puzzle books are on the table, his reading glasses, his Valium.

She knows he is all bluster and bluff: the way his hands tremble, he could never hold a rifle's bead. She wishes he would forget the dogs, wishes they would get in the car and go visiting like they did when they were younger. She recalls summer nights, late August, the wheat harvested, the soybeans and corn filling pod and husk, when he would drive her to the Bethlehem store for ice cream: Prairie Farms in a Dixie Cup, vanilla or strawberry swirl. How they would sit outside on the old Church of Christ pews, the women in their summer dresses, the men in clean overalls and caps, talking softly in the dark, chores done, and old Delbar Tapley rising, fiddle tuned, rosin gleaming on the cocked bow.

Who knew then Oren would get Parkinson's disease, would take Valium, but only half a tab for fear he might become an addict, just enough to help him sleep. And Glenna would sleep alone in a room across the hall, hear him at night shifting about in his bed until he gave up and shuffled to the living room to sit in lamplight working crossword puzzles or reading Carl Sandburg's biography of Lincoln — a good, true book, he has told her, about a decent man.

Tonight, he wears pajamas as yellow as lemon ice cream. "Rain coming." He shuts the door. "If it drops below seventy, I'll cut the A/C and open up the house."

"Leave it," she says. "Mercy. Don't let it trouble your soul."

They watch a program on television, a western, but not like the old *Gunsmoke* show. This one has robots in it: bionic gunslingers. They look so much like regular men, no one can tell they are indestructible, all circuits and wires. They keep terrorizing the town. No one, not even the brave sheriff, can stop them.

Oren says, well of course, that is all nonsense. "Just a made-up story," he says. "Not a word of it true."

Halfway through the program, their granddaughter Tess stops by with a box of Grandma Harp's Depression glass. "I want you to keep this for me," she says.

She is tall and slim-hipped with veins that kick and twitch in the papery skin around her eyes. She is wearing cowboy boots and tight Levis, and a tee shirt cut off at her navel.

"You ought to put on some clothes," Oren says.

"Me?" Tess laughs. "You're the one in your p.j.'s."

"Smart aleck," says Oren, and takes his flashlight outside.

Tess sets the box on the couch.

"I gave those dishes to you last Christmas," Glenna says.

"Granny, you know I won't have room for them in town."

"You'll have to make a place for them someday." Glenna squeezes her arm in what she hopes will pass for a playful gesture. "After we're both gone."

"Granny," says Tess, "how you talk."

Glenna has a frightening thought. "Promise me you'll never sell them, Tess."

"Why, Granny. Do you think I'd ever do that?"

Glenna would not be surprised, not one bit. Young ones . . . well, they are different is all she can say. She remembers how she and her mother cared for Grandma Harp. How the old woman, bedfast, lay in the dark, curtains drawn, bed table littered with medicines: camphor and castor oil, epsom salts and horehound. She called Glenna in each evening and asked her to sing hymns — "Blessed Assurance," "Bringing in the Sheaves," "Sweet Hour of Prayer" — and Glenna obliged, never once considered withholding her favor.

Now, as she examines the Depression glass, as she handles the thin saucers and plates, the pink glass etched with fleurs-de-lis, she remembers the name of the pattern is American Sweetheart. She imagines she will be the last of her family to know the name; even if she tells it to Tess, she fears she will forget it. She is certain Tess's mother, Joanne, does not remember, and she knows Joanne — who lives in Sweden and telephones twice a year: once on Christmas and once on Mother's Day — will never care for her or Oren when that time comes, nor will Tess.

At first this knowledge angers her, but as hard as she tries, she cannot muster an abiding malice. It is just the way it is done these days. The old ones are carted off to nursing homes. Their neighbor lady, Evangeline Harms, ended up there. Evangeline Harms who taught school for thirty-eight years — who fastened galoshes, and bandaged cuts, and swabbed Mercurochrome on scraped knees. In the end it didn't matter. In the end, Glenna knows, nothing you have done or been will save you.

She sees, through the picture window, the beam of Oren's flashlight jerking over her flower beds — marigold and zinnia in all their glory.

"How is he?" Tess asks.

If she dared speak the truth, Glenna would admit his balance is going; twice this month he has fallen, and his hands shake so badly she has taken to signing all his checks. But truth, in this case, is too humbling a confession.

She can recall the exact moment she knew they were old. A day last fall, when Oren, picking apples, asked her to steady the stepladder. "Hold fast," he told her. At the top, he reached his skinny arm out into the air, and she saw the pale flesh, loose on the muscle, chill and quiver. His hand shook as he groped for the apples, the Red Delicious, coddled them into the bushel basket resting on the ladder's top step. When he had finished, he stayed at the top, staring straight ahead. "What's wrong?" she asked.

"Just catching my breath," he said.

But she knew he was afraid to come down, afraid like a cat gone too far out a limb, and what was more, she was afraid for him. "Just step down," she told him. "Leave the basket. I'll get it later. Take one step. I'm holding on."

They have these secrets, facts they harbor, hints of their demise. They do not tell them to Tess, not even to their friends. They speak of them infrequently to themselves.

"Your grandfather is fine," she says.

Oren comes inside, sweat beaded on his lip. "I hear those dogs." He lays the flashlight on the table. "Sounds like off in the bottoms."

"Moad Keen's hounds," Glenna says to Tess.

"Took out three tomato plants last night," says Oren. "Night before, they were into the sweet corn."

"You can't stop those dogs." Tess takes his arm and helps him down into his recliner. "They just run where they want." Oren picks up the rifle and lays it across his legs. "Granddad," she says. "Quit acting the fool."

"Don't worry about me," he says. "You've problems enough of your own."

Tess and her husband Kenneth are losing their farm. The FmHA has foreclosed, and O. B. Ritchey, the auctioneer, has tagged equipment and livestock for sale. Tess and Kenneth are moving into town, into a double-wide trailer close to the garment factory where Tess is a seamstress. Kenneth, optimistic, as if some great load has left him, feels certain he can catch on with his cousin's building and remodeling business. He was never much of a farmer anyway, he says. Maybe it's all for the best.

Oren agrees. He could have given them money, enough to have kept them afloat, but that would have been a patch-up job, nothing that would have held. Better to let it go, he told Glenna, while they were young, with another chance, and time enough to take it.

What Oren does not know is that Tess has become involved with Spec Green, a DeKalb seed salesman, thinks she loves him — him with his eyeglasses, and his clean boots, and his big hands that smell of shelled corn. A secret she confessed to Glenna last spring on Decoration Day when they were setting coffee cans full of peonies on the family graves at the Gilead Cemetery.

"It's your business," Glenna told her.

"Oh, Granny. I feel so silly. Kenneth and I used to be locked together as tight as a dovetail joint. Now here I am, thirty-one years old, all loose at the hinges." She lifted her shoulders and let them drop. "I don't know a thing about love."

"Why, what a thing to say," said Glenna, unsettled by the fact that anyone dare question something so sacred. Wasn't the mystery the most of it? Still, it frightened her to think she herself had never before considered the carpentry of love. Had she missed something? She who had lived over seventy years. Had she not once, since the night she first met Oren at a

Methodist camp meeting, called to measure the braces and joists of their hearts?

"Don't worry," she said. "I won't tell your grandfather." Mismanagement of a farm, he could stomach, but barely. The immoral heart was, of course, another matter.

"Granny, you look after him," Tess whispers to her as she is leaving.

"You can't tell him anything," says Glenna. "Hardheaded. He'll do what he wants."

W H A T  H E wants is sleep, but tonight, like most nights, it shies away. He tries all the old tricks — drinking warm milk, counting sheep, remembering happy moments from his life — but nothing works. He has left the Valium in the living room, a last resort he will fall back on toward dawn, if need be. The digital clock Tess and Kenneth gave him last Christmas counts off the minutes, the numbers going *cl-clack* each time a new one flips over.

He has kept the air conditioner on, at Glenna's insistence, even though he cannot abide its drone. He would gladly sacrifice comfort to be able to open a window and listen to the night: the hot breeze rustling cabbage leaves and cornstalks in the garden, hungry hogs banging at the feeder lids, an owl somewhere far off in the hollow.

And what of the dogs? Moad Keen's hounds? When Oren last heard them, he could tell they had turned and were running east, back up toward the high ground. He imagines them swimming the Little Wabash, thrashing on toward the timber along the ridges, claws scrabbling over shale, water dripping from muzzles and bellies, the fox always before them, and Moad Keen creeping along the gravel roads in his pickup, listening for their calls: the bitch's bay, the pup's bullfrog *gump*.

How is it, Oren wonders, that Moad shoulders his life. A man never married, living alone in what used to be Hadley School a mile off the Sumner blacktop. A man who breeds mystery, rooting for ginseng the way he does, running his trotlines, curing pelts. A man people tolerate but never befriend. The one they hope never comes calling to ask a favor, to borrow a wrench, to hire out for work. Any lie — *I've got all the hay hands I need, Moad* — so obvious a sign he does not belong.

Oren tries to imagine a life without Glenna. He remembers his brother Jim dying in a veterans' hospital in St. Joseph, Missouri. He lived alone in a trailer park off the beltway, pumped gas at a Shell station, and drank. That was what people knew about him. But Oren, when he came to claim the body, could have told them much more: how when they were boys, Jim played harmonica, sang in the school Christmas pageant, received a certificate once for one hundred perfect spelling lessons. Those were the details he remembered, but he knew, even if he had the nerve to speak, the doctors would not have been interested.

They wanted to perform an autopsy. The thought of Jim cut and gutted seemed indecent, but the doctors said they could learn something, something that could help others, so Oren signed the consent form, a secret he has always kept from his sister and brother, something he still troubles over on nights like this when he cannot sleep. Was it the right thing? Does it matter now? He wonders if this is what naturally comes with age: a concern for decency, a fear of sin and offense.

And now these dogs set upon him like a curse. He would like to ignore them. Patience is a virtue, Glenna always says. But he has never been particularly Christian, not even now toward the end of his life.

A pain starts up his leg, an ache in his calf muscle. Too cool in the air conditioning, even beneath the sheet. He throws on a summer robe, sits on the edge of the bed, and fumbles in the dark for his house slippers.

In the kitchen, he drinks some water, leaning over the sink, his hand trembling. He uses a dish towel to wipe his chin.

He steps outside — a breath of air is what he needs. The wind is up, and between the rolls of thunder, he hears the hounds yelping somewhere in his woods, to the south, somewhere beyond the tree line, the pack of them, noses to the scent. Some twenty rods away, he gauges. And coming fast.

IN HER bedroom, Glenna is dreaming about Arizona. She is nineteen; Oren is twenty-one. It is 1937, and they have driven here on their honeymoon in Oren's father's Buick. They have driven all day to see the Grand Canyon and have arrived late in the afternoon. Still, the sun is glaring on the red sandstone. Daylight, this far west, will stretch on yet for hours.

Oren is in his shirt-sleeves; Glenna is in a summer dress, so white in the sun, it gleams. They have just shared the last Pepsi-Cola from an old metal cooler borrowed from Glenna's aunt, and the ice has melted, leaving a good three inches of water in the bottom.

"Watch this." Oren pours the water over the rim of the canyon, and they watch as it comes apart, separating into crystals that grow smaller and smaller, sparkling until they evaporate and disappear, not nearly halfway down.

She is dreaming all this when she hears the shot. At first she imagines the thunder has startled her. Then Oren is standing in the doorway, his shoulders slumped, the .30-.30 held in one hand, barrel down.

"Did you hear?" he asks.

"I heard."

A set of headlights sweeps over the wall, settling on Oren, whitewashing his face.

"I hit one. You didn't think I would." He leans the rifle against the wall. "It's done now, and I can't say I'm sorry."

The knock at the front door comes loud and explosive. They stare at each other, not speaking.

He wants to tell her he is afraid, not of Moad Keen whose hound lies dead in the barn lot, not of the Valium, not of the Parkinson's even, or of dying. No, it is something more than that, something more difficult to explain. A knowledge he has that these are their last days, that he does not believe in the soul, that what stops here — love, even its memory — stops. It is the loss of that, above all else, he mourns.

And Glenna is thinking she must remember to tell Tess that love, at long last, gives up its secret. Not in words she can pass along, only in a feeling as thin as a shiver, barely a whisper on a night she has been moving toward all her life: a night when she knows she has always been in the place she belongs. Patience, she will tell her. Stay with someone long enough. Stay until you are old.

She folds back the sheet and pats the mattress. Oren eases into bed beside her. They lie together, but do not touch, and while Moad Keen pounds on the door, neither knows that the other is recalling Arizona: how Oren poured water into the Grand Canyon, how it shattered like glass. They watched the last bits drizzle away until nothing was left — no proof, no sign. Enormous space below them, all that dry air.

"Like magic," Glenna said.

"No," said Oren. "It's more like something broke."

The rain comes. It falls in silver sheets. Falls over the fields and the river. Over the pup dead in the barn lot. Over Moad Keen who stands in the rain, whistling, shoulders pitched forward, waiting for someone to answer.

# THE PRICE IS THE PRICE

•     •     •     •     •     •     •     •

**M**Y BROTHER was a man named Leonard Salk, but in 1955 he was known as Buddy Day.

"All of a sudden he thinks he's a Gentile." In the dead hours of the afternoon, when it was only the two of us in the shoe store, my father would remind me what a traitor Lenny was. "Him with his bleached-blond hair and his fancy-schmanzy clothes. Cowboy boots, for Pete's sake. Somewhere in Heaven, your grandfather is cursing him. Your grandfather who sat forty-nine years of his life, curled over a shoe last, pounding leather, making an honest wage. Your grandfather, Julius Salk. A name we should all be proud of. *Salk.* An honorable name. Like the polio guy."

"Jonas," I said.

"That's right, Mr. Smarty-Pants."

The way my father saw it Jonas Salk had saved the shoe industry when he invented his vaccine. If polio still ran rampant, the fewer people there would be walking. And the fewer people walking — well, there you had it.

For some time, my father had been buying run-down businesses in the Negro district. All along Canal and Lincoln and Bellemeade, he snapped up furniture stores, discount appliance outlets, automobile dealerships. Some of these he remodeled. Then he staged gala reopenings. "Under New Management," he advertised, in order to attract speculators, usually other Jews, who bought the businesses from my father at a huge profit. But some of the businesses he kept so he could sell to customers who were anxious for credit. They would take one look at the sign in the window — "Nothing Down" — and sign contracts, agreeing to outrageous interest rates.

I was sixteen then, and I was my mother's child, eager and kindhearted. In my father's eyes, I had always fallen short of Lenny's *chutzpa*. But now that the two of them were on the outs, I had managed a newfound status.

"Sammy Salk," my father said to me shortly after Lenny became a professional wrestler. "Two *s*'s. That's got zip. That name means business. That's not a name you can forget."

Still, I envied my brother, the beauty of him. "Any dope can bite and scratch and gouge," he always told me. "It takes an athlete to really wrestle. Remember that, Sammy. Speed, balance, science." After his matches, he would be splendid in flannel slacks, vee-neck cashmere sweaters. I would watch him dress in the locker room. "Style," he told me, "is everything."

He did ads for Darmstadt's Department Store. There was a billboard on Highway 41: a life-size photo of Lenny dressed to the nines: a hounds-tooth sports coat, the collar points of his shirt folded over the lapels. The billboard said: "Take a tip from Buddy Day. Dress sharp, look sharp, be a winner."

Every time my father drove by that billboard, he started singing an Irving Berlin song, "Sadie Salome" or "Good-bye Becky Cohen." Once I joined him in a rousing rendition of "Yiddle on Your Fiddle."

"That's the spirit, Sammy," he said. "That's flushing the sand out of the old pipes. You and me should get an act together. *Salk and Salk.* We could play the Catskills."

We lived in Evansville, Indiana, a river city that had the edge and grit of industrial cities in the East I have since come to know. In winter, steam rose from the Ohio, and cranes, loading coal onto barges, squealed and crashed along the shore. At night, I listened to the tugs sounding their horns, long and lonely, and I imagined what it would be like to leave that city, to escape its ugly hold.

Downtown, coal dust streaked the buildings, and all winter a sharp wind came off the river and sliced its way through the business district. At Mesker Steel, the heat from the blast furnaces sent great clouds of exhaust rolling and fogging over the city, and when the wind was from the north, the stench from the stockyards and packing houses would fill my throat.

"We breathe bratwurst here," my father said once. "Is this a place for a Jew? I tell you, even the air will not let us keep kosher."

There were Jews in the city, but it was not a friendly place. The Germans who worked in the packing houses sometimes went loony and knocked over grave markers in the Jewish cemetery or splashed paint on the front doors of the synagogue. I never felt at home there, nor did my father, though we had moved away from downtown to a subdivision where the streets were wide and the lawns were green and the clanging and grinding of the city was far beyond us.

We had a new ranch-style home on Buena Vista close to the country club. On clear summer nights, we could hear the dance band — the heady brass, the raspy sax — and the applause at the end of a number, and if the night was particularly still, we might catch the sound of a woman laughing, and my father would say under his breath, as if he were trying to clear something from his throat, "*Goyim.*" That autumn, he had tried to join the country club, but Mr. Darmstadt — *the* Mr. Darmstadt of Darmstadt's Department Store — had personally returned his application, making it clear that he wasn't the sort of member the club wished to include.

A few weeks later, Lenny and a number of other wrestlers were invited to the club for an afternoon of golf.

"He'll probably wear a polo shirt," my father said. "Pink, I bet, with one of those green crocodiles stitched on the chest, like Eisenhower wears, or maybe yellow to match his bleach job."

LENNY LIVED downtown at the Sonntag Hotel close to the Coliseum. It was an arrangement that suited my mother, who believed all he needed was some time to get this wrestling business out of his system. Then, she said, he would settle down to the life God intended him to have — a teacher, or a writer, perhaps, someone who would make a living with his mind.

My mother was an optimist. For a while, she had been some-thing of a celebrity about town, "Miss Ruth" on Channel 7's kids' show *Ride the Reading Railroad*, but then the station manager had replaced her with "Miss Sandy," who wore bows in her blonde hair and resembled Doris Day.

"Your face is too severe," he told my mother. "You frighten the children."

"*Goyim*," said my father, but my mother refused to be bitter.

"There's a lesson to be learned in all this," she told me. "Remember, Sammy. By the inch, life's a cinch."

Three mornings a week, she repaired books at the public library. She mended cloth bindings, reinforced spines, erased obscenities smart-alecks had scrawled in the margins. Armed with her tape and scissors and glue, she sat at a desk and waged a war against the book carts stacked high around her.

"Pretty grim odds," I said to her once.

"Who am I to complain?" she said. "One by one, the job gets done."

On her kitchen windowsill, she kept tins for charities, each marked with its own label: "For Orphans," "For the Hebrew Home for the Aged," "For Milk for Jewish Children in Hospitals in the Old Country." Each Friday evening, she dropped a few coins into the *pushkes*. "You, too," she would say to my father, and he would grumble and fuss and reach into his pocket for a quarter or two. "Who are you to *kvetch*?" she would say to him. "Thank God you're not a pauper. A few good deeds you can stand. Me? I'm helping you store up *mitzvoth* so you won't have to die with a puny soul."

Her real talent was spending my father's money. "The Inspired Shopper," he called her.

"A toaster," she might say in the middle of a trip to the bank, as if some divine hand had anointed her with the idea, and off we would go to Darmstadt's Department Store in search of a Sunbeam toaster with avocado trim.

Clocks, candelabra, sling chairs: whatever caught her fancy, she bought.

My father never balked. "I can afford it," he would say when my mother came home with her latest purchase. "Let that hotshot Darmstadt know it. He should fall down on his knees and kiss your mother's feet. I tell you, he should give a rib to have her on his side."

He enjoyed a good pun, and when I was a kid, he used to break me up.

"Morton Salk," he would say to new customers, pumping their hands. "You've come to the right place. Take a load off. I'd say you're a 10C. Am I right, or am I right? Sure I am. You can trust me. I'm the Salk of the earth. Get it? Morton Salk. It's a pleasure to spice up your day."

What a jokester.

"Who's funnier?" he would ask me from time to time. "Me or Milton Berle?"

"You are, Pop."

"A Jew can be funny, Sammy. Here, listen to this one. A white man, a Negro, and a Jew are all given one wish each. The white man asks for securities, the Negro asks for a lot of money. But the Jew." Here he tapped his temple with his finger. "Do you know what the Jew asks for, Sammy?"

"What, Pop?"

"The Jew asks for some imitation jewelry." He started to sputter, his lips unable to contain the joy of the punch line. "Imitation jewelry," he said again. "And that colored boy's address."

ONE SATURDAY, after we had closed the store, my father said to me, "Okay, hotshot. Let's go. We'll grab some dinner, then we'll go to the Coliseum and see this great Buddy Day who used to be your brother."

Although there were no segregation laws in Evansville, by custom Negroes sat toward the top of the Coliseum, and on this night, before my father realized it, he had joined them there in the high bleachers. He took off his fedora and looked around at the black faces. I heard a man behind us whisper to a companion that Morton Salk was sitting in the bleachers. "You know. Morton Salk. His stores will give you credit."

A woman next to my father was waving a fan from a local mortuary. The fan said, "Eternal Rest." "You comfy, Mr. Salk?" The woman elbowed a skinny man sitting next to her. "Move over, fool. Give Mr. Salk some room to breathe. You want to make sure you've got the catbird's seat, Mr. Salk. This first match is going to be a lollapalooza. It's Buddy Day and Prince Cocoa Toussaint against those rascals, the Sheiks."

My father seemed humbled by the woman's gesture. He nodded to her. "Sammy," he whispered, "who is this Prince of Hot Chocolate?"

Prince Cocoa Toussaint, I explained to my father, was a colored wrestler Lenny paired with sometimes for tag-team matches. He was supposed to be West Indian royalty from Jamaica, but Lenny had told me he was really Harvey Meeks, a former steel worker from East Chicago. In the ring, he wore a gold lame cape and a crown he removed and set on a velvet pillow before the match began.

"A faker," my father said. "Like your brother."

My first night in the Coliseum, when I went looking for the locker room, I opened a broom closet by mistake and found Harvey Meeks crouched on a stool, his gold lame cape over his lap. He was trying to thread a needle so he could mend a rip in the cape, and when I saw him there, wetting the end of the thread with his lips, patiently trying to sight it through the needle's eye, I knew I had stumbled onto too much of the truth of him. He was a colored man who had to dress in a broom closet before parading into the ring, head steady and regal beneath his crown, a patsy on his way to be pummeled by white men, the same white men who refused to share their locker room with a "nigger."

Our eyes met, and he seemed to look at me as if he knew me. It was like a body slam. All the air went out of me, the way it did when the boys at school called me "sheeny" and "kike" — like they knew something about me, something true — and in that moment I despised Prince Cocoa Toussaint.

"Close the door," he said, and I did.

When he and Lenny came into the ring, the Negroes in the bleachers stomped their feet. They whistled and clapped their hands. The woman with the fan said to my father, "There they are. That's them. That's Buddy Day and the Prince."

The Prince was wearing his gold cape. He held it by the hem, and with a majestic flourish, he stepped between the ropes. Lenny braced himself on the turnbuckle and vaulted over the ropes, landing on his toes with an athletic bounce. His trunks were white, and his warm-up jacket was covered with silver spangles. "Buddy Day," it said across the back in gold letters.

When the Sheiks came into the ring, the Negroes jeered and booed. The Sheiks wore flowing headpieces and carried scimitars. Their chests were covered with pelts of black hair, and the toes of their wrestling boots swept up in devilish curls.

"Arabs," my father said. "Don't get me started."

They were actually two brothers named Joe and Dominick Regalbuto, Sicilians from Cleveland. They shared a room at the Sonntag Hotel across the hall from Lenny's, and on Saturday afternoons they listened to the Metropolitan Opera broadcasts on their radio. Sometimes I would hear them singing, and once Dominick came to my brother's room weeping. "Buddy, Buddy, Buddy," he said. "Once more, Mimi is finis."

The match began with Lenny displaying his athletic moves — flying head scissors, step-over toeholds, hammerlocks. And with each advantage he gained — with each grimace on the first Sheik's face — the crowd cheered, giving themselves to the old hope that on this night, at last, their champions, Buddy Day and the Prince, would triumph. The secret to a good match, Lenny had told me, was to see how much the wrestlers could make the fans believe. A good wrestler could convince the fans that anything was possible. "For a minute," he said, "we let them see what they want to see. We're shysters. That's us. Call us kings of the kindly deception."

But I couldn't be deceived. As I watched Lenny move the Sheik toward the corner, getting ready to tag the Prince, I knew what would happen next. While the Negroes around me came to their feet and even my father stood to see over the heads in front of him, I stayed in my seat, savoring the inside skinny Lenny had given me about the match's choreography and script. Even though I knew Lenny's matches were rigged, I took a certain pleasure in seeing him beaten.

I knew the Sheik would reverse the hammerlock and get the Prince in a choke hold and drag him to the corner, where the other Sheik would take over when the referee broke the illegal hold. In the meantime, Buddy Day would try to come to the Prince's rescue, but every time he entered the ring, the referee would chase him back to his corner, abandoning the Prince to further torment.

Finally, with superhuman effort, The Prince would break the choke hold and unleash his famous Cocoa-Butt. He would get each Sheik by the neck and bang their heads together. One would fall back and off the apron; the other would topple into the ring.

I closed my eyes and saw all this, and when I opened them, the Prince was going berserk. He had thrown back his head, and he was pounding his chest, and then he let loose a howl that chilled the back of my neck. The Negroes cheered louder, and I let their cheers lift me to my feet. The whites below us sat still, hushed, not sure how to react to the wild rousing around them.

Then the Prince reached into the waistband of his trunks and brought out a leather pouch full of voodoo dust, a black magic mojo that would bring the match to a swift and just end.

By this time, one Sheik was on his feet. The Prince dipped his hand into the leather pouch and flung the magic dust into the Sheik's eyes. The Sheik froze, and no matter how hard his partner tried to bring him around, he stood there like a zombie.

That's when the Prince tagged off and Buddy Day went to work on the other Sheik, catching him finally in a cradle hold and pinning him for the count. The Prince and Buddy Day lifted their arms in victory, and the crowd, both whites and blacks, roared.

My father shouted to me, "Did you see that? Did you see your brother kick that Arab's ass?"

Then the referee waved his arms over his head and shooed Buddy Day and the Prince back to their corner. He picked up the leather pouch the Prince had dropped on the canvas. He sprinkled what was left of the magic dust into his palm. He sniffed it and shook his head as if he had just gotten a dose of ammonia. Then he stepped into the center of the ring and declared the Sheiks winners.

My father didn't understand. "What?" he said. "Sammy, tell me. What's this mean?"

"They've been disqualified," I said. "They've lost. I could have told you that. It's all rigged."

"Lost?" my father said, and his voice was so weighted with disappointment that I was sorry I'd told him the truth.

The Prince and Buddy Day were leaving the ring, and as they made their way up the aisle, the Negroes around us clapped their hands — not wild, raucous cheering like before, but muted, reverential applause.

"They love them," I said to my father.

"That's more than love," he said. "Sammy, that's respect."

THESE WERE years of great moral dilemmas for my father. "Life's a real pickle, Sammy," he would say to me from time to time.

First, there were the Rosenbergs who were arrested in 1950 for espionage. Supposedly, they had passed secrets to the Russians about the atomic bomb, but there were many, like my father, who believed they were innocent victims of anti-Semites.

My father would weep as he read the tender letters Julius and Ethel wrote to each other while they were in separate cells at Sing Sing prison awaiting execution.

"Love," my father would say. "Is this not the important thing? Can no one see these are two people who love each other? And their two little boys. What will become of them?"

My mother marched in demonstrations for the Rosenbergs, took part in candlelight vigils. Whenever she asked my father to join her, his response was the same: "I have a name in the business world. I have customers who might not agree. You understand."

As much as he hated anti-Semites, he despised Communists. "Look at Stalin," he said. "Another Hitler." In 1952, Stalin had arrested a group of Jewish physicians. He had accused them of plotting the deaths of the Kremlin leaders. "He'll send the Jews to Siberia," my father warned. "Watch out for pogroms. Jewish blood will flow."

And all the while America was in the midst of the Red Scare. Senator Joseph McCarthy had engineered a witch hunt for Communists. They were everywhere, he assured us: our government officials, our teachers, our newspaper reporters, our neighbors.

"These are days that call for caution," my father said. "Especially for Jews. We should walk softly. We should know there are people who would call us Communists. Remember the Rosenbergs. Have mercy on their souls."

In 1954, during McCarthy's congressional hearings, Lenny came home with his blond flat top, his cowboy boots, his string tie, and he announced, from that day forward, he would be known as Buddy Day.

"If the world's out to get the Jews," he said, "why be a Jew?"

"Why be a Jew?" My father waved his arms in the air. "Because I'm a Jew. Because your grandfather was a Jew. Because Salks have always been Jews. You can't bleach that out of you, Goldilocks. You're a Jew. One day, you'll know that. Until then, may you grow with your head in the ground like an onion."

"This is what it means to be a Jew," Lenny said. "To rob the poor?" My father's business methods stuck in Lenny's throat.

"I make a good living, Mr. High and Mighty."

"Sure you do, Pop, but what does it cost you?"

These were the last days Lenny spent in our house before moving to the Sonntag.

My mother said to my father, "Bitter wine shrivels the tongue."

"Codes," he said. "Always codes and proverbs. Just once I wish you would speak a straightforward English sentence."

The night Lenny left us, I found my father in the kitchen warming a pan of milk.

"I'm thinking of a size ten loafer." He was sitting at the table, massaging his eyes with his fingertips. "Seamless sole construction, genuine leather uppers, cushion insoles, feels like you were born with it on, like you were walking on clouds. Sammy, Sammy, Sammy. You'd think God could arrange it so life would be like this."

THE NIGHT Buddy Day and Prince Cocoa Toussaint lost to the Sheiks, my father and I drove home through the Negro district. We drove down Bellemeade, past the shoe store, and turned onto Canal — a strip of blues clubs and billiard halls and barbecue joints. Down alleys, we could see figures crouched low, shooting dice, and on corners men huddled around fires burning in trash barrels.

My father turned down a side street, and soon we were driving by ramshackle houses so close they nearly sagged into each other. Old sofas sat on broken-down porches. A few Christmas lights blinked through windows covered with plastic sheeting, and their watery splashes of color made the gray houses seem all the more grim.

"Jesus," my father said. "How these people live."

When we lived on Riverside Drive, in the house where Grandfather Salk was dying, my mother would send Lenny and me to the drugstore for a bottle of Hadacol.

Hadacol, said Mickey Rooney, could work its magic on virtually any ailment. My mother believed it would cure my grandfather's heart disease, lower my father's blood pressure, and protect us all from cancer, fatigue, and the dreaded polio all mothers feared would strike their children.

I was eight then, and Lenny was thirteen. We were best chums, since our mother refused to let us have other friends. She drove us to school, and she was there each afternoon to take us home. The secret to avoiding polio, she said, was to stay out of crowds. "School you have to go to," she told us. "I can't have my sons grow up to be nincompoops. But never trade lunches, never drink from water fountains, and wash your hands every chance you get. Remember: better safe than sorry."

From time to time, we begged her to let us go to a movie, to a park, to the municipal swimming pool. She would press her hand to her sternum, take a breath, and roll her eyes to the heavens. "Fine," she would say. "Maybe this week there's a sale on iron lungs."

We knew she was talking about our neighbor, Andy Darmstadt — Kermit Darmstadt's son — who had polio. Sometimes, on our way to school, we would see his face turned toward the window, the swell of the iron lung around his torso. My mother would bite her lip. "There but for the grace of God," she would say, and Lenny would punch me in the ribs. As long as there was Andy in his iron lung, our fate as hermits was sealed.

One evening, when my mother sent us to the drugstore, Lenny turned in the opposite direction and said, "Come on."

It was just before supper, and in the dusk, I could see the faint outlines of Mr. and Mrs. Darmstadt moving by their lighted windows. The air was sharp with autumn's first chill, and all along Riverside Drive, I could smell soups and cabbages and chickens boiling and stewing.

Lenny had already reached the Darmstadts' stoop, and I hadn't moved. I remember watching him turn to me, pausing with one foot on the stoop, to see if I would follow, and even though I was afraid, I did.

Andy's mother was a timid woman. She opened the door just a crack.

"We've come to see Andy," Lenny said.

An eye blinked at us. Then Mrs. Darmstadt turned and called to her husband. "Kermit, it's those Salk boys from next door."

At the time Kermit Darmstadt did alterations at Schears Department Store, where my father managed the shoe department. When Mr. Darmstadt spoke, it sounded as if he had a mouthful of straight pins. "Let them in."

Andy had been our friend before he got sick and my mother refused to let us visit him.

"Andy's in the parlor." Mrs. Darmstadt motioned with her hand to a room off the entryway. "Go on in."

Right away, I decided the room smelled of polio — an odor of steam radiators and damp handkerchiefs. I closed my eyes and wondered how long I could hold my breath.

Andy lay by the window, taking in the last of the daylight. Heart-shaped leaves were dropping from the linden trees, and cars were moving along Riverside Drive. The sun had faded to a single violet streak along the horizon beyond the bend of the river. The iron lung was humming and whooshing, something inside it doing the work it was supposed to do. Lenny laid his hand on it, and I felt a cold shiver. "So this is it," he said.

Andy was staring up at us. He had a pale face and blond hair. His bangs were too long, and I wondered why his mother didn't cut them to get them out of his eyes.

"It's all pulsations," he said, sounding like a scientist. I could tell he was thankful for the opportunity. "Alternate high and low pressure. That's what keeps my lungs moving."

"We see you looking out your window," I said.

"That's right," said Lenny. "Our mother won't let us go anywhere. She's afraid we'll get it."

"We drink Hadacol," I said.

Andy smirked. "My mom gave me Hadacol until I wanted to puke."

I started to hiccup. I couldn't help myself. I hiccupped and hiccupped, and Lenny slapped me on the back and pinched my nose together and told me to breathe through my mouth. Finally Mrs. Darmstadt came into the room and snapped on the light.

"Goodness," she said. She poured a glass of water from the pitcher on the table. She held it to my lips. "Here," she said.

A few days later, Lenny told our mother that I had gone to Andy Darmstadt's house and drunk a glass of water.

"You let him do that?" she said. "Your brother? You're breaking my heart."

"Those people," my father said. "Krauts. What are they thinking?"

A few days later, Lenny and I were sitting on our stoop waiting for dinner when Kermit Darmstadt came down the street. He was in a rush, his stride somewhere between a walk and a run. He stumbled along; his topcoat, unbuttoned, flared and flapped about his legs. He passed us without looking our way, then stopped as if he had suddenly remembered us. He came back, and he said in a voice much louder than his normal way of speaking, "I've lost my son."

"Andy?" I said, even though I knew it was a stupid thing to say.

"Yes. Andy's gone. I was in the middle of taking in a suit coat, a very nice serge, and the phone rang, and it was Mrs. Darmstadt, you see, and she told me."

I sat there, my throat filled with cement. Then Lenny did something extraordinary. He went to Kermit Darmstadt, and he pulled his topcoat closed, and he buttoned it. He knelt and started at the bottom, working his way up, and when he got to the last button, Mr. Darmstadt closed his hand over Lenny's fingers. Lenny gently pulled free and buttoned the last button, and Mr. Darmstadt went on to his home.

"That was a goofy thing to do," I said to Lenny.

And Lenny shrugged and said, "His coat was unbuttoned. He looked cold."

For some reason, I was remembering all this the night my father and I drove home through the Negro district after the wrestling match. I was thinking about how much our lives had changed since the days on Riverside Drive. Grandfather Salk was dead, my father and Kermit Darmstadt were both rich, and Lenny was Buddy Day.

And my father had lost his faith. "Chosen people," he said to my grandfather when World War II was over, and we started to learn the atrocities of the Nazi death camps. "Hah! Chosen for what? The ovens? Money is what keeps the angel of death from the door. As long as you have money you can buy your way free from anything. Take it from me: God whimpers; money talks."

Now he stayed away from the synagogue and kept the shoe store open on Friday nights. "We're saving *soles*," he said to me once. "God doesn't run a tab in this store. No, sir. No charge account for him. If he walked in here right now, I'd tell him, 'Mister, you can pay as you go. Business does not know holy.' "

When we got home from the wrestling match, my father told my mother about Buddy Day and Prince Cocoa Toussaint and how they had stood up to those Arab lousebags the Sheiks. "Like Lot's wife," he said, describing the effects of the Prince's voodoo dust. "And the way the coloreds worshipped him. Our Leonard. Like he was a saint."

I WAS DREAMING of the Prince and Buddy Day when my father touched my face. "Wake up, honey," he said. "Listen to this."

A plan had come to him in the night: there was a property north of town, the old Deshee Farms, and it was going to be sold at auction on Thursday. "We'll buy it," he said. "All twenty-seven hundred acres. All that land. Won't that be something, Sammy?"

"What will you do with it?" I said, still dopey from sleep. "You're not a farmer."

"Here's the beauty of it," he said. "Mass-produced houses. Like Levitt did. You know? Levittown. Decent homes at a reasonable price. The only difference is we'll let coloreds in these houses. *Salktown*, we'll call it. We'll carve it in stone, and years later, there it'll be — our name known forever. I'm not like Levitt — a Jew who wouldn't do business with coloreds. Negroes have always been okay with me. Nigger pennies is still pennies, I always say. When it comes to cash, the only color is green."

It was barely dawn, but my father insisted we get in the car —

"pronto, Tonto" — and drive downtown to the Sonntag Hotel to give Lenny the news.

"He thinks he's the cherry on the sundae?" my father said. "Just wait until he gets the lowdown on this."

By the time we reached the Sonntag, my father had sold me on Salktown. We had driven by Lincoln Gardens, the public housing project, and he had stopped the car and said, "What does everyone want, Sammy? A house of their own. Something they can be proud of. That's what we'll give them. God bless us."

Lenny was in his boxer shorts, and his eyes were narrow with sleep. He sat on his bed, rubbing his face, while my father paced back and forth, describing the scheme.

"Picture this," he said. "We'll build forty houses a day. I've studied up on this."

I was sitting on the bed next to Lenny, and I tapped his knee with my finger. "That's right," I said. "We've studied up on it."

All around us, magazines and newspapers cluttered the room: the *New Republic*, the *Negro Digest*, the *Daily Worker*, *I. F. Stone's Weekly*, the *Carolina Israelite*. After years of listening to Lenny's lectures on social issues, it gave me a great joy to play the big shot.

"We'll make everything simple," my father said. "Concrete floors, composition Sheetrock walls, no basements. Who needs a basement? Hey, Sammy?"

"I'll tell you who." I tapped Lenny's knee again. "The dope who wants a place to store the junk he'll never use."

"That's who," my father said.

Lenny lifted his face. "Houses? Why are you telling me about houses?"

"You'll want in on this," my father said. "I saw the way the coloreds worshipped you. *Buddy Day*. I've seen that billboard on the highway. The hell with Darmstadt. You come in with me. 'Take a tip from Buddy Day: No down payments, no closing costs, no secret extras. At Salktown, the price is the price.' Hey, that'd make a great slogan. 'The Price Is the Price.' I just thought that up. It's got pizazz."

"You saw me?" Lenny said.

"At the Coliseum," I said. "Me and Pop."

My father sat on the bed next to Lenny and put his arm around his shoulders. "Get this," he said. "We'll bring the assembly line to the building site. Nonunion workers. A group to lay the foundation, another to frame the walls. Bang, bang, bang, you've got a roof. Zip, zip, zip, you've got wiring. Rub-a-dub-dub, you've got plumbing."

"Just like clockwork," I said.

Lenny got up and walked across the room to his dresser. He leaned over to look at himself in the mirror. "I'm a wrestler." He rubbed his hand over his flat top. "Why would I want to build houses? It sounds like another scheme of yours to make dough. You want to make me a thief like you?" He turned away from the mirror and stared at my father, his hands on his hips.

My father stared back, but addressed me. "Sammy, what does everyone want?"

"A house of their own," I said. "Something they can be proud of."

"You think the coloreds worship you now, Leonard?" My father stood up and drew his shoulders back. "Just wait until you sell them a decent home. Our margin of profit will be very small. Hell, we might as well give these houses away."

I remembered Lenny's exit from the ring the evening before, how he and Prince Cocoa Toussaint had made their majestic march down the aisle accompanied by the Negroes' respectful applause. Just before he left the arena, he stopped to lift his arm in a salute, the way a king might acknowledge his subjects. He had always been vain. At home, he would spend hours in front of the mirror, posing and flexing, telling me the name of each muscle: bicep, tricep, pectoral, deltoid. He had it down to a science. "When you look good, you feel good," he told me. "You should get in shape."

"Listen to your brother," my father said once. "Look at him, a regular Charlie Atlas. Muscles in his earlobes. He'll make it big in business some day. Mark my words, Sammy. He's got what it takes — moxie, no shame."

I knew I would never have a body like Lenny's. I could spend years in the gym, but I would never look like that. I had my father's body — short and squat — and I moved with his apish gait. I could feel his life in my muscles, never the life Lenny had. When we walked down the street, I would catch Lenny turning his head, ever so slightly, to glimpse his reflection in store windows. And he would glance at strangers, making sure they were staring at him.

"You like that, don't you?" I said to him once.

"Like what?"

"The way people stare at you."

"Sure I like it," he said. "Wouldn't you?"

So I wasn't surprised when he started getting dressed. "All right," he said. "Maybe I can keep you honest. We'll get some breakfast. Then we'll drive out there. Just to take a look."

DESHEE FARMS had been a resettlement project devised by the Federal Subsistence Homesteads Corporation, one of Roosevelt's New Deal programs. The deal was this, my father said as we drove up Highway 41 to give the place the once over. Back in the thirties, when farmland in south-central Indiana had been ravaged by erosion and floods, the government had started looking to move those farmers and their families to more productive soil. That's where Deshee Farms came in. Twenty families moved there in 1938 and lived there free — "Not a cent," my father said — in exchange for their sweat. "Dairy cows," my father said. "Chickens, hogs, all that Old McDonald stuff. What else do they have on a farm, Leonard?"

"Oranges," Lenny said.

We had stopped at a roadside stand and bought a bag of oranges some bumpkin had brought up from Florida, and now Lenny was eating one. He was peeling it with his thumb, and sometimes the juice sprayed up into my face. From time to time, he would tear off a section for my father. "Man, that's sweet, Sammy," my father said once. "That is the juice of Heaven."

Our car was filled with the smell of that orange, and Lenny and my father were really going to town. They were working those wedges around their mouths, smacking their lips, rolling their eyes with ecstasy. You'd have thought they were going to die from that orange. They loved it so much they were in agony.

"Here, Sammy," Lenny said to me. "Give it a try. Go on. You don't know what you're missing."

"We don't grow oranges in Indiana," I said. "I defy you to show me one citrus farm in this entire state."

"Apples," he said. "We grow apples. And peaches. Right, Pop?"

"Cantaloupes," my father said. "Watermelons."

"And tomatoes and wheat and corn," said Lenny. "And what else, Pop?"

"Houses. We're going to grow houses. Salktown."

Brother, they were full of themselves.

"Beans," I said. "You're beans and hot air. Both of you."

My father spit a seed into his hand and dropped it into the ashtray. "Mr. Grumpy Butt," he said. "Mr. Party Pooper. What is it you have a problem with? Can you tell me that?"

I didn't know. Not exactly. I only knew it had something to do with Salktown, and the way we all puffed up like toads when we talked about it. You'd have thought we were saints — some sort of goddamn geniuses for having come up with the scheme — like we expected the world to come running to us and kiss our hands.

When I took a good look at us, I got the same feeling I did when I went to the wrestling matches. Like I had entered a world where everyone lived secret lives. Lenny was Buddy Day, Joe and Dominick Regalbuto were The Sheiks, Harvey Meeks was Prince Cocoa Toussaint. That world was easy. Everyone knew everyone else was a fake. It was this world that was starting to give me problems, the world we were moving through just then in my father's Oldsmobile, the three of us washed in the scent of oranges, while outside it was winter. The highway was blanched white with the cold, and the trees were bare, and I could feel the wind buffet the car.

"I don't feel good," I told my father.

"Eat an orange," he said. "Vitamin C. You'll feel better."

At Deshee Farms, we walked over the frozen fields, out past the barn and the chicken coops and the twenty or so deserted frame houses. The project had gone belly up, my father said, because people hadn't wanted the government to run their lives.

"People want to own a house," he said. "A plot of land. Something they can take pride in. That's what we'll give the coloreds. Hey, Leonard?"

"How much do you figure we'd have to go?" Lenny asked.

"Fifty an acre. I figure we can get it for that. Maybe seventy-five. No more."

My father started marking off a lot, walking a straight line, counting his paces, then turning on his heel, his short arms swinging with each step. I thought of newsreels I had seen of Nazis goose-stepping in Germany.

"You know what they used to call this place?" My father shouted to us. "Hitlerville. Hey, how about that? A Jew buys Hitlerville and sells it to the blacks."

ON OUR WAY back to town, we stopped at a steak house for lunch.

"I made up a little joke the other day," my father said. "Something to amuse myself. Perhaps you'd like to tell it, Sammy?"

I shook my head. "You tell it, Pop."

"It goes like this," my father said. "A Jew is riding the subway when he sees a Negro reading the *Jewish Daily Forward*. 'Mister, I don't want to be rude,' says the Jew, 'but I have to know. Are you Jewish?' The Negro lowers the paper in disgust and says . . . tell them what the Negro says, Sammy."

"Pop."

"Tell them."

I cleared my throat. " 'Jewish, *oy*. That's all I need.' "

"Get it?" my father asked.

"I get it, Pop," Lenny said.

"Colored *and* Jewish," my father said. "Now that's a double curse."

We ate awhile in silence. Then my father decided to school us in the art of promotion.

"If you've got a product," he said, "you've got to sell it. You've got to give it pizazz. Take this broccoli, for instance." He speared a floret of broccoli from my plate and held it aloft on his fork. "How do you like it, Sammy?"

"It's all right."

"All right won't cut it," he said. "It's boffo. Go on. Say it. Say, 'This broccoli is boffo.' "

I bowed my head over my plate. "This broccoli is boffo."

"I can barely hear you. Punch it, Sammy. Make me believe it."

Lenny grabbed the fork from my father's hand and said in a loud voice: "This broccoli is by-god boffo."

"Atta boy, Leonard." My father leaned back in his chair. "Now you're talking. Stick with me, son. Me, Morton Salk." He patted his chest. "Trust me. I've got plans."

THAT EVENING, at dinner, my mother said to me, "What's your opinion of this Rosa Parks?" She liked to keep up on current events. "Come on, Einstein. Think. Alabama. Montgomery. The bus boycott."

I shook my head. "I'm not up on it."

Rosa Parks, my mother told me, was a Negro who had refused to stand in the back of a bus. She had been arrested for violating the city's public transportation laws.

"There's a boycott," she said. "The Negroes aren't riding the buses. They've organized car pools, they ride bicycles, many of them walk."

"Now there's some wear on shoe leather," my father said. "Yes, sir. A man could sell some shoes in Montgomery, Alabama."

SOON THERE was a new *pushke* on my mother's windowsill: "For Negroes in Montgomery, Alabama."

She had gone to the local chapter of the National Association for the Advancement of Colored People to find out where donations could be sent. "A kind gentleman gave me the address of a minister in Montgomery," she said. "He was very polite. Very well-mannered. A gentleman named Meeks."

"Harvey Meeks?" I asked.

"I don't know," she said. "With him I wasn't familiar. He told me his name was Mr. Meeks. That's all I know."

"Meeks," my father said. "It's not a good name for business. A man could not do business with that name."

"Business." My mother waved her hands in disgust. "With you it's always this business."

My father took a twenty dollar bill from his wallet. He folded it and put it into my mother's *pushke*. "There, how do you like that? How's that for business?"

"It's a start," she said. "Who knows? There might be something good to you yet."

THERE WAS a time when my mother insisted we celebrate the Passover. *Pesach*, my grandfather called it, the Festival of Freedom. The year he died, my mother prepared a family seder feast. I remember the *matzo*, the bitter herbs, the roasted egg and bone. I remember the *charoseth* — its fragrant apples and cinnamon and wine, and the way my father sat at the head of the table, propped up by pillows.

These were the days of my father's guilt. "Don't be like me," he told me once. "A needle in your father's heart. I wouldn't keep holy. I wouldn't be a *frummer* like your grandfather. Now he's gone. God forgive."

As the youngest child at the table, it was my place to ask the *Fier Kashehs*: "Why do we eat unleavened bread? Why do we use bitter herbs? Why do we dip the herbs in salt water? Why do we recline at the table?"

My father answered with the story of the Israelites' bondage in Egypt and how the Pharaoh refused to let them go. "Ten plagues afflicted the Egyptians," my father said. "Let's see. Oh, yeah. Red Sea parts, Israelites am-scray, at Mount Sinai they get the Torah, etc., etc. The end."

At the end of the seder, my father poured a goblet of wine to leave for the Prophet Elijah. I remember how his hand began to tremble, as if suddenly this was all too much for him, and my mother reached across the table to help him. When she touched his wrist, the decanter bumped the goblet, and it tipped over, and the wine spilled out onto the tablecloth.

"Enough!" My father's voice exploded. "You touch me and I come apart. My father's soul doesn't live in me. It won't fit."

For some time, my mother had believed in the transmigration of souls. "You think the dead are dead? Pish. Once a soul, always a soul. Sammy, there's no telling who we're carrying around inside us."

She had grown up in the County Children's Home, and still, she said, she could sense another Ruth — the Ruth she would have been had she known her parents. This other Ruth was out there somewhere — a spirit swirling, and without it, *this* Ruth, the one I called my mother, would never know completely who she was.

She said this to me the night my father put the twenty-dollar bill in the *pushke*. He had gone into his den, and I was helping her with the dishes. Later, we went into the living room, and she read the newspaper. "Sammy," she said. "It's the darndest thing. Come look."

She was studying a picture of Rosa Parks. Mrs. Parks was standing on a street corner, her purse held demurely before her. She looked bookish and shy in her round gold-rimmed spectacles, and there was something Asian in the delicate bones of her face.

"I look like her," my mother said. "Don't you think?"

My mother's features were mannish: a square jaw, a nose too large for her face, thick eyebrows that grew together if she didn't keep them plucked. *Severe*, like the station manager at Channel 7 had said. Toward the end of her reign as Miss Ruth on *Ride the Reading Railroad*, she had stood before the hall mirror practicing her smile. She had taught me how to massage her face to relax the muscles and give her a more pleasant look. I can still recall the feel of her hard cheekbones, the line of her jaw, the indentations at her temples. My fingers were shy on her face. "Press harder," she always had to tell me. "Go on. I won't break."

She looked nothing like Rosa Parks, but I told her she did.

THE NEXT morning, she was standing in the middle of the living room, hands on her hips. She was wearing a business suit: a tailored skirt and a short jacket with a sensible brooch pinned to the lapel. She drew her shoulders back and gave a tug to the bottom of her suit jacket, as if she had decided something.

"Sammy," she said. "Look at that clock." She pointed to a sunburst clock she had bought a few weeks before at Darmstadt's Department Store. "The six is off-center. Do you see it? It doesn't line up with the twelve. Every time I look at it, I feel all out of whack. Sixes and sevens, Sammy. Do you see what I mean?"

"Yes," I said. "Maybe. I'm not sure."

"I cannot live another minute with that clock." My mother clapped her hands together. "Take it down."

By the time I had taken down the sunburst clock, my mother had found a chip in a lamp. The lamp's base was a matador figurine. "Feel." She took my finger and rubbed it over the matador's fanned out cape. "You see? Who needs this junk? Back it goes."

I felt no chip in the matador lamp, and, to me, the six on the sunburst clock lined up perfectly with the twelve. But I didn't say anything to my mother.

"Negro women in Alabama are walking miles in the rain to

clean white women's homes," she said. "And here I am spending money on kitsch I don't need. Grab the lamp, Sammy. We're cleaning house."

When my father came out to his Oldsmobile, I was crammed into the back seat along with the sunburst clock and the matador lamp.

"Ruth?" my father said.

My mother was in the front seat, her hands folded in her lap. "I have errands," she said. "The six is off-center," I told my father. "There's a chip in the lamp."

Said my mother, "Take me downtown."

All the way downtown, my father tried to talk my mother out of returning the lamp and the clock.

"What will Darmstadt think?" he said. "That we've hit on hard times. That's what. He'll spread the word. 'Morton Salk is knocking on the gates of the poor farm.' "

"Fiddle," my mother said.

At the corner of Fourth and Lincoln, my father pulled to the curb. "I will not drive another inch," he said, "until you stop this nonsense."

My mother snapped at him. "You think I'm too good to ride a bus?"

"Wouldn't that be fine?" My father pushed his hat back on his head. "Morton Salk's wife on a bus."

My mother opened the door and stepped out onto the curb. She gave another tug to her suit jacket.

"Well?" she said.

My father turned off the ignition and folded his arms across his chest. "Sammy, tell your mother I'd rather pull this Olds-mobile downtown with my eyeballs than be a party to her cock-amamie scheme."

Minutes later, I was on a bus with my mother. The bus was full, so we stood in the back: she with the sunburst clock, I with the matador lamp.

"Your father will get over this," she said. "You did the right thing."

I wasn't so sure.

We had been doing so well, my father and I. He had drawn me into his confidence, made me a partner of sorts. He had shown me how to measure feet, how to use a shoe horn, how to say, "You look like a million bucks in those wingtips. Yes, sir, you look like an uptown sort of guy."

The secret to selling, he had told me, was to make the cus-tomers feel special. "People are dying to spend their money," he had said. "All you have to do is give them a reason. Make them feel like they can't live without what it is you got to sell."

He had convinced me I could be somebody — a man re-spected for a practical skill, a man of shoe polish and leather. I could give the world something it could use.

And now I had ruined all that because I felt sorry for my mother.

At Darmstadt's, my father was waiting for us. He was standing near the returns counter, his hat in his hands.

"Who's minding your store?" my mother asked him.

"The store will open when it opens," he said. "So what some-one buys his loafers somewhere else."

Just then, Mr. Darmstadt walked by. "Such a pleasure," he said. "The Salk family. Making some exchanges, are we? I trust you're not dissatisfied."

"Returns," my father said. "You're selling shoddy goods, Darmstadt. Just look at this clock. The six is all cockeyed from the twelve. And this lamp. Show him, Sammy. A chip in the base."

Mr. Darmstadt waved away my offer. "No need for proof," he said to my father. "Your word is good with me."

MY FATHER and I dropped my mother off at the library, and once we were alone in the car, he said to me, "Your grandfather was a shoemaker. He left his mother and father in the *shtetl* in Russia and came to America. In the Depression, when no one bought shoes, he became a cobbler. And when that wasn't enough and still our stomachs roared, he sent me down the alleys to look for produce the grocers had tossed into the garbage. That's my story. That's what I want you to remember about me. I was the age you are now, and I stuck my hands into garbage for a rotten peach, brown lettuce, black bananas — anything I could take home for my family. May you never know such hunger, such disgrace. The world will give you nothing but bitter sausage." His voice was a fierce whisper. "Take all you can, Sammy. Promise me. Yes?"

THAT AFTERNOON, my father left me to watch the shoe store while he and Lenny went out to talk to contractors. All morning, I had done my best to avoid him, and I was glad to be alone.

I was turning what he'd told me over in my mind when Prince

Cocoa Toussaint came into the store. He was wearing dark glasses, and he kept them on. It gave me the willies. I couldn't see his eyes, and I imagined he was watching every move I made.

"I'm looking for an oxford," he said. "Something suitable for walking."

"Walking?" I said. "Yes, sir. I've got just the thing. I'd say you're a 10D. Am I right, or am I right?"

"Why don't you measure?" He sat down in one of the customer chairs and propped his foot up on a stool. "Just to make sure."

He was a 10D, and it made me feel pretty good to guess his size, but sad, too, because I saw myself turning into my father.

"How about that?" I said to Prince Cocoa Toussaint, but I couldn't muster much enthusiasm. All of sudden, I didn't want anything to do with my father's shoe store. "Now we're cooking. An oxford. 10D. Coming right up."

The oxford, he said, was too tight.

"Right." My father had taught me never to question a customer. "We'll try a 10½."

Prince Cocoa Toussaint kicked off the shoe. "I'm out of the mood for an oxford. I'd rather have a loafer. Do you sell loafers here?"

"A loafer," I said. "Yes, sir. Size 10½."

The loafer, he said, was too loose.

"A 10," I suggested.

"No. I'd like a wingtip. Something dignified, don't you think?"

In the ring, he would taunt his opponents with his voodoo dust. Will I fling it now? Now? Now?

"Size?" I asked.

"That's your job. You decide."

I brought a 10 and a 10½. The 10 was too small. The 10½ was too loose. I tried to make a joke: "How about a 10¼?"

"Try this on for size, little man. One day I'm walking down an alley. Listen to me, now. This was in East Chicago. The slums. I'm talking folks like the kind your daddy gets rich from. Folks like the ones who come in this store. You with me?"

I was sitting on the shoe stool, my shoulders slumped, and he was bending over me, those dark glasses reflecting the lights above us.

"Slums," I said.

"That's right. And you know what I see? A chalk circle on the cement. A circle, no bigger than this." He curled his hands and touched his fingertips together. "And there's another circle farther on, and another, and another, all kinds of these white circles, getting smaller and smaller. At the end of the alley, I see a policeman, down on his hands and knees, drawing the smallest circle with his chalk, and I say to him, 'What's the story?' 'A man got shot,' he says. 'A black man?' I ask, and he looks at me and says, 'What do you know about it?' 'What do you know about it?' he says, and I look back down the alley, down that trail of white circles, and I want to tell this policeman I know everything about it, everything about how the white devil gets his hands around the black man's throat, chokes the life out of him, bleeds him dry until all that's left is a single speck of blood, but I can't because now I'm a suspect. There, little man, walk around in that for a while and tell me how you like it."

By the time he finished, his voice was trembling and his chest was heaving, and I thought of how he would go berserk in the ring. He put the fingertips of both hands together in another circle. He squatted down, and stared at me through its lens.

"Now, what I want to know is this," he said. "Is it true what I hear about this Salktown? This Garden of Eden for black folks? Your daddy and your brother playing God? They got their chalk out? They ready to draw circles around our blood?"

"No," I said. "You've got it all wrong. No down payments, no closing costs, no secret extras. The price is the price."

It was easy to fall into my father's rhythm, to copy his spiel, and the more I talked about mass production — about holding down costs and making decent housing affordable for all — the more I began to believe in Salktown. I could see it: rows and rows of clean, simple homes, tidy lawns, Negro children jumping rope on the sidewalks. I could see women watering flowers, men reading newspapers on shady patios.

And then Prince Cocoa Toussaint said, "This sounds like Heaven: a house any man can afford. But that house has to have a couch, and it has to have a refrigerator, and where do you think these folks will buy all that? From good Massah Morton Salk, of course. Not once will they think about his killer interest rates. Rich get richer, little man, and all the while your daddy and brother will be patting themselves on the back because they did such a good turn for the niggers."

The word had never sounded as ugly as it did in the mouth of Prince Cocoa Toussaint.

"That night in the Coliseum," I said. "When you were sewing

your cape in the broom closet. I was the one who opened the door."

He laughed. It was a wicked, deep-chested laugh, bubbling with anger and grief. "You think you were scared then?" he said to me. "Little man, just wait."

WHEN LENNY and I were kids, we would argue over pieces of candy our grandfather gave us. "*Fen dibs*," my mother would finally shout. Half to each.

There were no *fen dibs* when it came to the *pushkes*. Once, when my mother caught me stealing coins from the tins, she told me that my greed would keep an old widow hungry, that there would be one less tree planted in Israel thanks to me.

A few minutes after Prince Cocoa Toussaint left, she came into the store.

"Lonesome Sammy," she said.

I was standing at the cash register tossing a quarter into the air, and when she said my name, I dropped it on the counter. She slapped her hand down on top of it. "*Fen dibs*," she said.

Next to the cash register was a display stand featuring a pair of open-toed pumps, a preview of the new spring fashions. When my mother slapped her hand down on the quarter, the pumps fell to the counter. They landed upright, one of them slightly ahead of the other, as if they had stepped from the display stand and were pausing a moment before going on.

I watched my mother's face light up. I remembered how she used to practice her smile in a mirror when she was Miss Ruth on

*Ride the Reading Railroad.* She looked from the pumps to the shelves and shelves of shoes in my father's store.

"*Fen dibs,*" she said with a laugh.

I imagined my father and Lenny talking with contractors. They would rattle on and on about Salktown. They would draw diagrams, calculate costs.

"Are you serious?" I asked my mother. "Do you mean it?"

She leaned across the counter. "All right," she said. "What do you have in mind?"

IT WAS SIMPLE.

"You think I don't know how to call a shipping company?" I said to my mother when she started to lose her nerve. "You think I don't know invoices, bills of lading?"

"All right," she said. "You know."

"Just tell me where."

She took a slip of paper from her pocketbook. "That's the name. Reverend Johns."

"Montgomery," I said.

"That's right. Montgomery, Alabama."

IT WAS LATE, and my mother and I had been waiting in the kitchen. "You sent them where?" my father said when he came home.

He paced to the sink and rested his arms on the counter. His shoulders sagged as if the weight of this were more than he could bear. I got a picture of him then, rummaging through garbage as a boy, and for a moment I was sorry for what I had done.

"All of them?" He straightened and turned to us. "Everything?"

"Yes," my mother said. "Every pair."

"Sammy? You let your mother do this?"

"It was my idea," I said.

"You?"

I nodded. "Every pair."

LATER THAT NIGHT, my mother and father woke me, and made me swear to keep the secret.

"For Salktown," my father said. "A good cause."

"A *mitzvah* for your father," my mother said. "Please, Sammy. God save him."

I dressed in the dark, as if any light might open my eyes to what we were about to do. My father took a bucket of black paint from the garage and we drove to the shoe store. On one window, with large, sloppy brushstrokes, he drew a swastika, and on the other window, in a jagged scrawl, I wrote the words: *Hitler Didn't Finish the Job.*

BY MIDMORNING the next day, the word had spread through the Negro district that Morton Salk had sent all his shoes to Montgomery, had *given* them, out of the goodness of his heart, to the people who were walking miles and miles every day because of the bus boycott. And look, said the Negroes who stood on the sidewalk in front of the store, look what someone has done?

"Who would do such a thing, you ask?" My father stayed

outside the store all day. "I'll tell you who. Nazis. Hatemongers who would want the Jews and the Negroes dead."

This, he told me, was good public relations. "Sammy, what a turn you've done me. That shoe stunt was brilliant. Oh, sure, it'll cost me at first, but look at it as an investment. An investment in Salktown. Like hotcakes I'll sell those houses. Me, Morton Salk — a man of the colored people. Hell, we'll make up the loss in no time."

"The world's getting ready to explode," Lenny told me when he saw the swastika on our father's store. "I can feel it. All hell's getting ready to break loose. A Texas death match: no holds barred, no disqualifications. You don't want to be a dummy when that happens. Trust me. You want to know where you stand."

So, for the time, I stood with my father and my brother. "Three Salks," my father said that day. "Ready to make a few simoleons. Right, Leonard?"

"Right, Pop."

THAT AFTERNOON, Kermit Darmstadt drove by the store. He stopped his Cadillac in the street and honked his horn. It was a polite honk, just a tap, to catch Lenny's attention.

"Look who's here," my father said to the crowd of Negroes. "Darmstadt. A kraut. Did you ever see his prices? How many shoes do you think he's sent to Alabama?"

"I better see what he wants," Lenny said. "Don't worry, Pop. I'll handle him."

I watched Lenny put his hands on top of the Cadillac and lean over to speak with Mr. Darmstadt. After a while, he straightened and waved his arms in the air. I heard Mr. Darmstadt race the motor, and when he pulled away from the curb, his tires squealed.

"What's his story?" my father asked Lenny when he came back to the store.

"Business," Lenny said. "That's all."

Mr. Darmstadt had found out about Salktown. "He wants me to put the kibosh on the whole plan," Lenny told me later. "If I don't, he says he'll make sure I never wrestle again. Buddy Day? Kaput."

"What are you going to do?"

"Hey, I'm with Pop. I'm going to build houses."

I went with him to the Coliseum and helped him empty his locker. I stuffed his gym bag with his high-topped wrestling shoes, his crew socks, his jockstraps, rolls of Ace bandages, bottles of body liniment, the hypodermic syringes he used to drain blood from cauliflower ears. He folded his shiny white trunks and the warm-up jacket with silver spangles and "Buddy Day" in gold letters across the back.

It came to me then what Buddy Day had meant to him: a chance to be the darling, the fair-haired boy, the bearer of hope and decency in a world of brutal deceit. And now he thought he would find that in Salktown.

I had been prepared to let him be hoodwinked, but now I saw what it would cost him.

"It was me who sent those shoes to Montgomery," I said. "Me and Mom."

Lenny laid the warm-up jacket on the bench. "That Hitler crap on the windows?"

"Pop," I said. "It's all a scam."

THE AUCTION was held that Thursday at the county courthouse. My father had bought a new suit, a three-piece navy pinstripe, and a new hat, a black homburg.

"Darmstadt's?" I asked.

"A man has to look good," he said, "on such an important day."

At exactly eight o'clock, we left the house and drove to the Sonntag Hotel. I watched my father's hands on the steering wheel. He drove with such care I felt it in my stomach, an ache for the boy he had been. In the set of his hands, small and curled, I could see his entire life.

"This is a beautiful day, Sammy," my father said to me. "The sun is shining, I'm wearing good clothes, I'm driving a nice car — listen to that motor hum — and I'm on my way to pick up my son. Yes, sir. This is the kind of day a man could make a name for himself."

At the Sonntag Hotel, Lenny didn't answer my father's knock. He knocked and he knocked, and finally a door opened across the hall, and Dominick Regalbuto stuck out his head and said, "Buddy Day. Poof. He's gone."

My father stood there as if he had caught a faceful of Prince Cocoa Toussaint's voodoo dust. He pushed his glasses up onto his forehead, and with the tips of his fingers he rubbed his eyes. "Sammy," he said, "what does this mean?"

I remembered the night we went to see Lenny wrestle, how my

father had been suckered in, how he had rooted for Buddy Day, this *goy* my brother had become. And even though the idea of Salktown might have started as a scheme to win Lenny back to the family, I could see in it, that morning at the Sonntag, my father's enormous capacity for hope.

"He's probably waiting for us," I said. "He probably got antsy and took a cab. You know him."

"Sure," my father said, smiling. "That's the story. Your brother. He was always a real go-getter."

THE AUCTION began at nine o'clock in the courthouse rotunda. Sunlight was slanting through the windows, falling across my father and the other men who had gathered there, farmers in corduroy jackets and clean overalls. They stood with their caps in their hands, shuffling their feet and speaking in hushed tones.

"Look at these rubes," my father said. "We'll get this for a song."

Then Kermit Darmstadt emerged from the crowd. He was wearing a camel hair topcoat, a single red rose pinned to one lapel. He tapped my father on the shoulder with the gold knob of his walking stick. "Pity about your store, Salk."

"I didn't know you were interested in farmland," my father said.

"Twenty-seven hundred acres would make a good golf course, don't you think?"

"Mr. Hoity-Toity," my father said to me when Mr. Darmstadt had moved away from us. "He thinks the world needs another golf course. Don't worry, Sammy. We'll get that land. We'll get it on account we're doing the right thing. Do you see your brother anywhere?"

"He'll be here," I said.

My father opened the bidding at twenty dollars an acre. One of the farmers countered with twenty-one, and my father quickly raised it to twenty-two. A few other farmers made hesitant offers, but when my father had placed the bid at fifty dollars an acre, they fell quiet.

Kermit Darmstadt stood a few feet away from us along the curve of the rotunda. He kept his eye on my father, watching without a hint of a smile or a frown. I remembered what Lenny had said once about the bus boycott in Alabama and the passive resistance techniques Dr. Martin Luther King had learned from Mahatma Gandhi.

"There's an art to it all," Lenny had told me. "This passive resistance jazz. The way I see it, you have to make yourself stone. No matter if some cop is shoving you around with a billy club, or calling you 'nigger this' or 'nigger that,' you have to keep yourself under control. Never let that sonofabitch know how much he's hurting you. Not like in the wrestling game, where every time the bad guys lay a hand on you the promoter expects you to gasp and come up all rubber-legged and look like a goddamn idiot when there's nothing in the world wrong with you. I'd like to go down there to Alabama. I'd like to let one of those cops crack me with his club. I'd just stand there. I wouldn't even grunt."

The secret, he said, was knowing you were better than the other guy but never saying a word about it. Just letting your enemy come to that conclusion and enjoying the sick look on his face when he knew it, and when he knew you knew it.

"Fifty dollars once," the auctioneer said. "Fifty dollars twice."

Kermit Darmstadt raised his walking stick. "Fifty-five dollars," he said.

My father shifted his weight from one foot to the other. "Sixty," he said.

"Sixty-five," said Mr. Darmstadt, and the farmers backed away, making a space in the rotunda for him and my father.

"Seventy," said my father.

"Seventy-five."

"Eighty."

"Eighty-five."

"Ninety."

"Ninety-five," said Kermit Darmstadt.

I heard my father mutter under his breath, "Sonofabitch." He turned his head, searching for Lenny. His eyes were wild and frightened, and I thought of Lenny when he was caught in a choke hold, straining and straining for the Prince's hand, and just when he got close, the villain would drag him away.

I knew my father was in trouble. When he looked around the rotunda and didn't see Lenny, it was like all the life went out of him. I remembered the summer nights when we listened to the dance bands at the country club until my father finally shut the windows, and still the music and the laughter came to us as if from some far-off, imagined place.

My father put his hand on my shoulder, and I felt his weight shift to me. "Sammy," he said, and I knew I had been waiting for this moment all my life, for this chance to save him.

"Ninety-five once," the auctioneer said. "Ninety-five twice."

My voice rang out brilliant and clear in the sunlit rotunda. "One hundred dollars," I said.

I felt my father's hand squeeze my shoulder.

"One hundred and five dollars," Kermit Darmstadt said.

I loved the feel of the words on my tongue: "One hundred and ten."

"Sammy," my father whispered. "Ix-nay. I can't swing it."

But by this time I was in love with the sound of my voice, with the chant I had entered into with Kermit Darmstadt.

"One hundred and twenty," he said.

"One hundred and thirty."

I couldn't stop myself, and finally my father rallied. When Mr. Darmstadt bid one hundred and forty, my father bid one hundred and fifty.

"And sixty," Mr. Darmstadt said.

"And seventy," said my father.

He was shouting now, his voice filling the rotunda. He was jabbing his finger in the air, and his new homburg had fallen to the floor. His eyeglasses had slipped down on his nose, and when he barked out his bids, his cheeks bellowed out, red and shiny with sweat.

"Two hundred," said Mr. Darmstadt.

"Two-fifty," shouted my father.

I closed my eyes and listened, and when it was finally done — "Five hundred dollars," my father said — I was giddy with the glorious madness of it all.

My father was panting for breath; his hands were shaking. "Did you see that, Sammy?" he said. "I nailed that bastard. Oh, Jesus. I really did."

OUTSIDE, in the car, my father tried to pull himself together. "Five hundred an acre," he said. "Let's see. That's five hundred times twenty-seven hundred acres. How much is that, Sammy?"

"One million three hundred fifty thousand," I said.

He tipped his head back and closed his eyes. "That's scary," he said. "That is a goddamn scary figure. But don't worry. I'll call in some favors, swing some deals. Oh, I really nailed that sonofabitch Darmstadt. I nailed his ass to the wall." He opened his eyes and started the car. "Come on. I've got to make some calls."

At the shoe store, he parked in the alley, and we went in the back door. "So I'll sell a few businesses," he said. "I've got prospects. I've got a list as long as my arm. I'll just get on the telephone and start the ball rolling. 'You want to make a few bucks?' I'll say. 'Just buy this furniture store. I've got a clientele built up here. The name Morton Salk means something in this neighborhood. Why not let me make you a rich man?'"

I left him alone in his office and made my way through the store past the empty shelves and display stands. Outside a crowd of Negroes had gathered on the sidewalk in front of the store. They were listening to Prince Cocoa Toussaint who was standing on top of a car parked at the curb. He was wearing a shiny black suit and a narrow tie, and when he spoke, his voice boomed out rich and deep, the ringing blast of a steel furnace.

"It won't be *Salk*-town," he was saying. "It'll be *Soak*-town. And you'll be the ones getting drenched. How much do you pay in interest now? Sure you've got your television sets and your washing machines, but look at what it's costing you. What makes you think this Salktown will be any different? Nothing is ever going to change until we make it change. Look at what's happening in Alabama. We can do that here. All it takes is a boycott. Don't buy the white man's goods. Don't pay his interest rates. He'll come around quick enough. Even Morton Salk. Even a Jew like him."

"But he sent those shoes to Montgomery," someone in the crowd said.

"Those shoes?" said Prince Cocoa Toussaint. "You want to know the story about those shoes?"

He crouched down to help someone onto the roof of the car. It was Lenny.

"It's all a PR stunt," he told the crowd. "Everything. The shoes, the swastika. He's just trying to make a good name for himself."

"Listen to him," someone said. "That's Buddy Day."

"No." Lenny held up his hands as if he were surrendering to something he had known all along. "I'm Leonard Salk. I'm Morton Salk's son."

Just then, my father came to the front of the store. He was whistling, and he walked with a swagger, his hand jangling the coins in his trouser pocket. "Good news, Sammy. Great news. I've got fish on the hook. Everyone knows a good deal when they see one. They all want to buy a business from Morton Salk."

The crowd was roaring now, and Lenny was waving his arms in the air.

"What is it?" My father stood at the window, looking out

between the jagged bars of the swastika he himself had painted. "What's he saying?"

For some reason I thought of Andy Darmstadt before he came down with polio. He didn't know about iron lungs yet. He didn't know he would die on an October afternoon.

My mother was an orphan; she had never learned the first, true part of herself. All we didn't know lay in wait for us, ready to spring, the way the Sheiks would ambush Prince Cocoa Toussaint and pummel him in the corner.

"Sammy," my father said again, "what is it? What's your brother saying?"

I told him the truth. "He says he's Leonard Salk. Don't you hear him?"

My father pressed his hands against the glass.

"Listen," I told him. "He says he's your son."

●　　●　　●　　●　　●　　●　　●　　●

LEE MARTIN was born in Illinois. He earned his M.F.A. from the University of Arkansas, and his Ph.D. from the University of Nebraska-Lincoln. His stories have been widely published in journals including *The Georgia Review, Story, DoubleTake, New England Review, Yankee, Prairie Schooner,* and *Glimmer Train Stories.* He received a Nebraska Arts Council Master Award Individual Artist Fellowship in Fiction (1995), as well as Individual Artist Fellowships in Fiction from the Ohio Arts Council (1987) and the Tennessee Arts Commission (1989).